✦RICHARD PAUL EVANS✦

THE ROAD TO

race

THE THIRD JOURNAL OF *THE WALK* SERIES

SIMON & SCHUSTER

NEW YORK   LONDON   TORONTO   SYDNEY   NEW DELHI

Simon & Schuster
1230 Avenue of the Americas
New York, NY 10020

Copyright © 2012 by Richard Paul Evans

First Simon & Schuster hardcover edition May 2012

SIMON & SCHUSTER and colophon are registered trademarks
of Simon & Schuster, Inc.

For information about special discounts for bulk purchases,
please contact Simon & Schuster Special Sales at
1-866-506-1949 or business@simonandschuster.com.

The Simon & Schuster Speakers Bureau can bring authors
to your live event. For more information or to book an event,
contact the Simon & Schuster Speakers Bureau at
1-866-248-3049 or visit our website at www.simonspeakers.com.

Designed by Davina Mock-Maniscalco

Manufactured in the United States of America

1   3   5   7   9   10   8   6   4   2

Library of Congress Cataloging-in-Publication Data
Evans, Richard Paul.
The road to grace : the third journal of the walk series / Richard Paul Evans.—
1st Simon & Schuster hardcover ed.
      p.   cm.
1. Executives—Fiction. 2. Life change events—Fiction.
3. Walking—United States—Fiction. 4. Loss
(Psychology)—Fiction. 5. Diaries—Fiction. I. Title.
PS3555.V259R63 2012b
   813'.54—dc23   2012004985
ISBN 978-1-4516-2818-0
ISBN 978-1-4516-2833-3 (ebook)

✦ ACKNOWLEDGMENTS ✦

I would like to thank those who have made this book possible.

First, my lovely and wise daughter Jenna, who travels Alan's route with me, figuratively and literally. You're a great travel companion, sweetheart—a true saunterer. Thank you for all your help. I couldn't do it without you.

To my sweetheart, Keri. For your support, friendship, love, wisdom, and goodness. I'm grateful for you.

To Laurie Liss—friend, confidant, secret agent.

To all my friends at Simon & Schuster: Carolyn Reidy, for keeping the house in order and for all your support over all these years and all these books. Many more thanks to come. To Jonathan Karp. I enjoy working with you, Jon. Thank you for your attention to this series as well as your input and creativity. To my new editor, Trish Todd. Thanks, Trish. I look forward to years of working together. You have a comforting spirit. (Also to Molly, your supernatural assistant, thanks for being so remarkably competent, cheerful, and dependable.) And Gypsy da Silva. I adore you, Gypsy. We need to do Little Brazil again.

Mike Noble and Noriko Okabe in S&S audio. You make the marathon sessions survivable.

My staff: Diane Glad, Heather McVey, Barry Evans, Karen Christoffersen, and Lisa Johnson.

Acknowledgments

The Christmas Box House Staff and Board.

Also, some friends who have made a difference in my life this year. Karen Roylance. Glenn Beck. Kevin Balfe. Shelli Tripp. Judy Bangerter. Patrice Archibald. The Students of Riverton High School—go Silver Rush!

As always, my dear readers. Thank you for your loyalty and goodness. There is no magic without you.

✶ To my big brother, Dave. I still look up to you. ✶

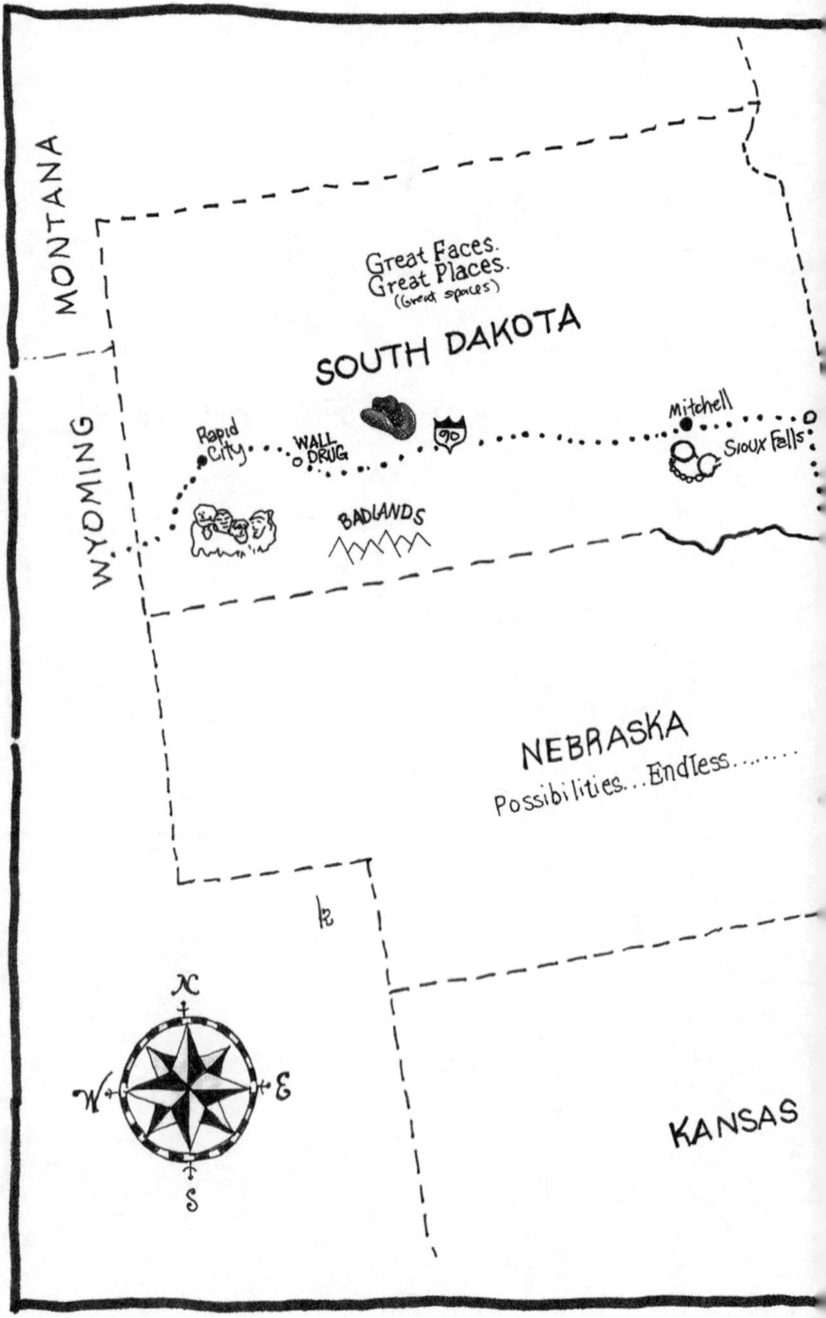

MONTANA
Great Faces.
Great Places.
(Great spaces)
SOUTH DAKOTA
WYOMING
Rapid City
WALL DRUG
90
Mitchell
Sioux Falls
BADLANDS
NEBRASKA
Possibilities...Endless........
N
W
E
S
KANSAS

HAND-DRAWN MAP FROM ALAN
CHRISTOFFERSEN'S ROAD DIARY

MINNESOTA

IOWA
Is this heaven?

Des Moines

Omaha

Sidney (Half Way there)

Lincoln

ILLINOIS

St Joseph

Hannibal

MISSOURI

ST. LOUIS

If you are going through Hell, keep going.

—*Winston Churchill*

THE ROAD TO

Grace

PROLOGUE

I had a dream last night
that McKale came to me.
"Where are you?" she asked.
"South Dakota," I replied.
She stared at me without speaking and I
realized that she didn't mean my location.
"I don't know," I said.
"Keep walking," she said.
"Just keep walking."

Alan Christoffersen's diary

A few years ago I was walking through a Seattle shopping mall when a woman at a kiosk peddling discounted airfare shouted to me, "Sir, if you have a minute, I can save you nearly half on your travel!"

"Thank you," I politely replied, "but I'm really not interested."

Undeterred, she asked, "If you could go anywhere in the world, where would that be?"

I stopped and looked at her. "Home." I turned and walked away.

I suppose I'm as unlikely a candidate to walk across the country as you could find. I was never one who, as Steinbeck wrote, was afflicted with "the urge to be someplace else."

That's not to say I haven't traveled. I've done my share of it and I have the passport stamps to prove it. I've seen the Great Wall of China, the Hermitage in Russia, and the Roman Catacombs. Truthfully, all that travel wasn't my idea. My wife, McKale, wanted to see the world, and I wanted to see her happy. Actually, I just wanted to see her, so I went along. The foreign locales were just different backdrops for my picture of her.

Her. Every day I miss *her.* I may be a closet homebody, but life has taught me that home was never a place. Home was *her.* The day McKale died, I lost my home.

Up to the moment I lost McKale, I had lived my life as a liar. I don't say that just because I was in advertising. (Though that qualifies me as a professional liar.) Ironically, I was annoyingly honest in unimportant matters. For example, I once went inside a McDonald's to return a dime when the gal at the drive-in window gave me too much change back. But I deceived myself about the things of greatest consequence. I told myself that McKale and I would be together until we were old and gray—that we were somehow guaranteed a certain amount of life before our time expired, like cartons of milk. Perhaps a certain amount of self-deception is necessary to get one through the day. But whatever we tell ourselves, it doesn't change the truth: our lives are built on foundations of sand.

For those of you just joining my journey, my childhood sweetheart, my wife, McKale, broke her back in a horse-back riding accident, paralyzing her from the waist down. Four weeks later she died of complications from her accident. During her last days, while I was caring for her, my business was stolen by my partner, Kyle Craig, and my financial world collapsed, leading to the foreclosure of my home and repossession of my cars.

With my wife, business, house, and cars gone, I contemplated taking my life. Instead, I packed a few things, said good-bye to Seattle, and started my walk to the farthest walkable distance on my map: Key West, Florida.

I suppose if I were completely honest with myself (which I've already established I'm not), I'd have to admit that I'm not really walking to Florida. Key West is as foreign to me as any of the towns I've walked through on the way. I'm walking to find what life may hold. I'm looking for hope. Hope that life might still be worth living, and hope for the grace to accept what I must live without.

Perhaps that's true of all of us. I'm certainly not alone in my quest to find that grace. There are others I have met on my journey. Like the elderly Polish man in Mitchell, South Dakota, who took me in; a young mother I stayed with in Sidney, Iowa; the old man I met in Hannibal roaming graveyards in search of his wife; and the woman I met as I walked out of my hotel in Custer, South Dakota. This is their story too.

Again, welcome to my walk.

CHAPTER

One

One can never know what
a new road will bring.

Alan Christoffersen's diary

Custer, South Dakota, is a tidy little tourist town near Mount Rushmore and the Crazy Horse Memorial. I spent two days in Custer, convalescing after a long and emotionally challenging stretch through eastern Wyoming. Sunday I was ready to resume my journey. It was a cool May morning and I rose with the sun, showered, and shaved. The luxuriousness of my temporary surroundings was not lost on me. In the weeks ahead, crossing through the barren stretch of South Dakota's badlands, I would be without a soft bed and hot water.

I laid my road atlas open on the bed and studied it for a few minutes, drawing a path with my finger. Then, once I was committed to a course, I marked it in pen. My next target was thirteen hundred miles away: Memphis, Tennessee, by way of St. Louis. From Custer I would walk north until my path intersected with Interstate 90, then I'd walk east through South Dakota, through the badlands, about four hundred miles to Sioux Falls.

The night before I had washed five pairs of my socks in the hotel sink. They were all gray and threadbare and due to be retired. Unfortunately, they were also still damp. I put them in the dry-cleaning sack from the hotel closet and packed them into my backpack. Then I put on my sweat-stained socks from the day before, laced up my shoes, and headed out of the hotel.

As I walked through the hotel's lobby I noticed a woman sitting in one of the chairs near the reception desk. She had gray hair, though she looked too young to be so gray. She wore a long, black woolen coat, and a burgundy silk scarf tied around her neck. She was beautiful, or had been once, and something about her was hard to look away from. Something about her looked familiar. Peculiarly, she was likewise watching me with an intense gaze. When I was just a few yards from her she said, "Alan."

I stopped. "Excuse me?"

"You *are* Alan Christoffersen?"

As I looked into her face I was certain we had met before, but I couldn't place her. "Yes," I said. "I am." Then I realized who she was.

Before I could speak she said, "I've been looking for you for weeks."

CHAPTER

Two

There are people such as Benedict
Arnold or Adolf Hitler, whose names
become synonymous with evil and
more adjective than proper noun.
For me, "Pamela" is such a name.

Alan Christoffersen's diary

The woman was McKale's mother.

"Pamela," I said. It was a name I had never spoken without pain or anger—and usually both—a name that seemed to me, as a boy, and even as an adult, to represent everything wrong with the world. Pamela was the source of McKale's greatest angst—a permanent sliver in her heart. There's a good reason that I hadn't recognized her immediately. I had met Pamela only once before, briefly, at McKale's funeral and had said all I ever intended to say to her then.

"What do you want?" I asked.

"I was hoping to talk to you," she said.

"About what?"

She swallowed nervously. "Everything."

"Everything," I repeated. I shook my head. "No. We have nothing to talk about."

She looked upset, but not particularly surprised by my response. "I don't blame you, but I've come a long way . . ."

I looked at her for a moment then lifted my pack. "So have I." I turned from her and walked out the hotel's front door.

The town of Custer was bustling with tourists and the traffic was brisk, the sidewalks along Mount Rushmore Road crowded with those who had come to see the monument. I planned on walking about twenty miles that day and I was ready for breakfast, though, admittedly, seeing Pamela had somewhat dulled my appetite.

I couldn't believe she had come looking for me. *What could she possibly want to talk about?* After I had walked about a hundred yards from the hotel, I looked back. To my dismay Pamela was following me, walking about a block behind me on the same side of the street. She wore a sun visor and had a large pink bag draped over her shoulder.

Half a block later, I stepped into the Songbird Café—the restaurant the hotel clerk had recommended.

The café was small and crowded and the waitress had just seated me at a round table in the corner when the bell above the door rang and Pamela walked in. She held her bag in both hands and glanced furtively at me as she waited to be seated. Fortunately, the hostess led her to a table on the opposite side of the room, where she stayed. I was glad that she didn't come to my table. I would have left if she had.

I wolfed down my breakfast—a tall stack of buttermilk pancakes with two fried eggs, three strips of overdone bacon, and a cup of coffee. I paid my bill, then slipped on my heavy backpack and walked out. Pamela was still sitting at her table, sipping coffee, her dark eyes following me.

I crossed to the other side of the street and walked several blocks back toward the hotel, turning in the middle of town at the 16 Junction. I followed the highway north toward the Crazy Horse Memorial. There was more than one route to I-90 from Custer, but 16 would lead me back by the monument, which, if not a shorter route, seemed more interesting.

When I got to the top of the hill above Custer I glanced back at the town. Unbelievably, Pamela was there, walking a quarter mile behind me. I shook my head. Did she really intend to follow me? I doubted that she was in the physical condition to keep up with me. She didn't even have the shoes for it. If she thought I was going to stop and wait for her she was sadly mistaken.

The first three miles from the city were mostly uphill and Pamela quickly fell back until I couldn't see her anymore. Less than a half hour from Custer she was nowhere to be seen. I wondered what McKale would have thought of the situation. The mother she had spent her life longing for was chasing me.

Four miles out of Custer I reached the *Avenue of the Chiefs*. I was still enamored with Korczak's work (will forever be), so I took a short detour and walked up to the park entrance. There's a ten-dollar admission fee to the park, and I didn't have the time or inclination to walk all the way to the monument, so I just stood at the entrance and admired the work from a distance. I wondered if the massive sculpture would be completed during my lifetime. I hoped so. Even as an old man, I would definitely return to see the finished piece. Suddenly my heart ached. The idea of growing old without McKale filled me with intense loneliness. I turned back toward the highway and resumed my walk.

The road after Crazy Horse was mostly steep downgrade with wide shoulders and only a few buildings along the way, including a business offering helicopter rides to the monuments.

I stopped in Pennington County and ate lunch out of my pack. I had an apple, a granola bar, and a slightly smashed ham and Swiss sandwich I had purchased the day before at the grocery store in Custer.

As I ate, my thoughts returned to Pamela—along with my anger. I wondered how far she had walked before she had turned back. I also wondered how she had found me. After a few minutes I pushed her from my mind. The thought of her following me overwhelmed me with disgust. I finished eating then got back on the road.

The next few hours were ideal walking conditions— smooth, new roads with black asphalt, wide shoulders, clean air, and a beautiful mountain setting—something I appreciated more after my long walk through the desolation of eastern Wyoming.

The sun had begun its decline when I heard a car pull up behind me and roll to a quick stop, gravel crunching beneath its wheels. I turned around to see an aged, turquoise Chevy truck with a matching camper top, stopped about fifty feet behind me. The passenger side door opened and Pamela stepped out of the vehicle. She said something to the driver, then swung her bag over her shoulder and continued walking after me. I groaned. *She's as persistent as McKale*, I thought. Maybe persistence is genetic. If McKale wanted something she didn't stop until she got it.

After the truck drove away, Pamela shouted to me. "Alan, we need to talk."

"No, we don't," I shouted back without looking. "Just leave me alone." I hurried my pace. When I reached Hill City an hour later she was nowhere to be seen.

CHAPTER

Three

I don't know if poltergeists or ghosts
exist, nor do I care. There's too much
I don't understand about the world
I inhabit for me to worry about a
world I haven't been to yet.

Alan Christoffersen's diary

During its brief heyday, Hill City was nicknamed "Hell City" or "One Mile of Hell," since there was a church on each end of town with fifteen saloons in between them. The city was established during America's centennial celebration of 1876, and was originally a mining town, only the second to be settled in the Black Hills.

Hill City was about twenty miles from Custer, most of the way downhill, which may seem an easier walk, but I was feeling the descent in my knees, which were throbbing. Darkness was falling when I started looking for a place to spend the night.

On Hill City's main road I came upon a hotel called the Alpine Inn, a quaint, Bavarian-styled building with gingerbread trim and a wood-planked porch. Above the front stairway was a sign that read:

Fine European Lodging

I walked into an empty bar scattered with small round tables. To the left of the room was a door that led to a restaurant, which was surprisingly crowded. A woman standing near the restaurant's entrance was watching me from behind a burled walnut reception desk. She smiled as I approached her. "Good evening," she said.

"I'd like to look at your menu," I said.

"No need," she said. "We only have one item on our menu. Actually, two. Filet mignon, small or large."

At first I thought she was joking but her expression remained serious. "Really?"

She nodded. "I know, it's unusual, isn't it?"

I had never encountered a restaurant like this, but judging from how crowded the place was, they appeared to be doing something right.

"I'll have the filet mignon," I said.

"Good choice," she said. "Right this way, please."

She sat me at a small table near the room's back, inner wall. There were paper menus in a stand on the table, which, considering the restaurant's limited selection, seemed a little odd.

A moment later my waitress appeared. She was a tall woman probably my age, with blond hair and a prominent nose.

"I'm Heidi," she said. "Large or small?"

"Large."

Not surprisingly, she didn't write anything down. "Would you like something to drink?"

"Do you have juice?"

"Apple, orange, and cranberry."

"I'll have some apple juice. Can you mix that with cranberry?"

"Absolutely. One cranapple."

"And some ice water."

"Of course."

Before she walked away I asked, "Do you know if your hotel has any vacancies tonight?"

"No, but I'll check."

A minute later she returned with my juice. "Here you are. And I checked on our rooms. Unfortunately, we don't have any vacancies. We only have four rooms."

I frowned. I had been looking forward to staying there. "Do you know of someplace else nearby I could stay?"

She thought for a moment. "I'm pretty sure there's a bed-and-breakfast about a half mile north of here. It's called the Holly something. Holly Inn, I think."

"Along the highway?"

She nodded. "If you keep heading north you won't miss it."

"Thank you," I said. "I'll check it out after I eat."

✦

My meal was brought out quickly—another benefit of a limited menu. The filet mignon was served with a lettuce wedge, homemade ranch dressing, and buttered Texas Toast.

"Is there anything else you need?" Heidi asked.

"No," I said. "Are you always this busy?"

"Year round. The hotel is busy too. The rooms are nice." An impish grin crossed her face. "Haunted, but nice."

"Haunted?"

"Yes, but I probably shouldn't tell you that."

"How do you know they're haunted? Have you ever seen a ghost?"

"No. But one of the other waitresses said she did."

"And you believe her?"

"She's never lied to me before. Besides, it's not what she said, it's how she said it. It happened in the middle of a busy Friday night. She was in the employee restroom behind the kitchen. While she was washing her hands she looked in the mirror. There was a woman dressed in eighteenth-century clothing standing right behind her. We all heard her scream.

"I went to see if she was all right and she was pale and shaking. She looked like she was going to faint. She quit on the spot. I ended up taking all her tables. She's never set foot in here since." She looked at me, studying my reaction. "Anyway, I better let you eat before your dinner gets cold. There's more about the hotel on the back of the menu. Bon appétit."

I cut into the steak. The meat was masterfully prepared and so tender that, had I been inclined, I could have cut it with my fork. I took a few bites then lifted the menu. The hotel's history was printed on the back, and I read as I ate.

Hill City was a placer gold mining town, founded during the western gold rush. Its success was short-lived, and the miners quickly moved on, leaving the town to two residents—a man and his hound.

In 1883, the town experienced another boom when tin was discovered, and an English mining company invested millions organizing the Harney Peak Tin Mining, Milling, and Manufacturing Company. The company built the inn—then named the Harney Peak Hotel—as a luxurious residence for the mining executives. Like the town's previous mining venture, the tin rush didn't last very long, and the town died again, until Mount Rushmore resuscitated the area, bringing in tourist gold.

In 1974, a German woman named Wally (pronounced Volley) Matush bought the Harney Peak Hotel and renamed it the Alpine Inn. By then, ghost sightings had become commonplace and the new management wasn't shy about telling their guests that the hotel was haunted. Wally even requested to be buried under the hotel when she died so she could walk the halls with the other ghosts.

Reading about hauntings made me think about Pamela. I wondered what had happened to her since I'd left her behind. For the first time since she'd shown up, my anger had settled enough that I could objectively examine my feelings. In spite of my rage, I felt somewhat conflicted about the situation. Part of me felt that even talking to Pamela was a betrayal of McKale. Another part, perhaps a more civilized part, thought it wrong to not at least let her say what she'd come so far to say.

I pushed the conflict from my mind. Right or wrong, I had no desire to talk to her. If she was hurting, so be it. She had brought this on herself. McKale owed her nothing. I owed her nothing.

I finished eating, paid the bill, then picked up my pack and headed north up the main road in search of the bed-and-breakfast. I stopped at a small market on the way and stocked up on water and supplies: Pop-Tarts, apples, trail mix, salami, oranges, protein bars, jerky, a baguette of hard crusted bread, and a few canned items: soup, chili, and stew.

I asked the cashier if she knew anything about the bed-and-breakfast, but, disconcertingly, she had never heard of it. I wondered how that was possible in a town of this size. I went back outside and continued to walk, worrying that I had unwittingly passed by the house in the dark. I had walked another mile before I came to a sign on the side of the road that read:

The Holly House
A Bed and Breakfast Resort

I wasn't sure where the resort part came from, as the place looked more like the Brady Bunch house than a fancy resort. The building was lit outside with flood lamps, revealing an exterior decorated with holly leaves and wreaths.

I walked around the house and knocked at the side door. I was met by a middle-aged woman who I assumed was the "resort's" owner.

"May I help you?"

"I need a room for the night."

"Welcome," she said, smiling broadly. "My name's Dawna. Come in."

I stepped inside what looked to be the home's living room. The room had dark red shag carpet and forest green walls, covered with framed prints of Christmas-themed watercolors.

"What's your name?" she asked.

"Alan."

"Pleased to meet you, Alan. We have five rooms available and a cabin out back. I'll show you around and you can tell me which room you'd like."

"Are your rooms haunted?" I asked.

She looked at me with a strange expression. "Not that I know of. Did you need a haunted room?"

I grinned. "No. Unhaunted is fine."

Dawna led me through all five of the rooms, beginning with the Western Room, which featured a replica of Wyatt Earp's revolver, the USA Room, the Bridal Suite, the Harley Room (undoubtedly patronizing the annual motorcycle event in Sturgis), and the Victorian Room, which was decorated with Dawna's mother-in-law's christening dress and a working, antique Victrola.

The rooms all looked nice and I didn't care much about which room I stayed in, so I selected the Western Room for the pragmatic reason that it was closest to the front door. That and I liked its tub, which was just about large enough for a cowboy *and* his horse.

"Fine choice," Dawna said. "For breakfast tomorrow I'll be serving my *festive* breakfast casserole. What time do you think you'll be wanting to eat?"

"I usually get an early start," I said, pleased at the offer of something festive for breakfast. "Maybe seven. Possibly earlier."

"I'll have breakfast waiting for you. Have a good night."

I went to my room and turned on the television while I let the jetted tub fill. The television was tuned to a reality show about people bidding on the contents of abandoned storage units. *They should do a show about a guy walking across America*, I thought. *Just not me.*

I turned off the television, undressed, then soaked in water hot enough to turn my skin red until I was ready to go to sleep.

CHAPTER

Four

To say that one doesn't know when to
quit is either an insult or a compliment,
depending on the outcome.

Alan Christoffersen's diary

The next morning I woke to the sound of dishes clanking in the dining room. I checked the clock. It was nearly eight o'clock. I showered, shaved, and dressed, then packed up and went outside my room for breakfast. Dawna walked into the dining room about the same time I did.

"Good morning, sleepyhead. Glad I got up at five-thirty to get breakfast on."

"I'm sorry. I . . ."

She waved her hand. "I'm just joshin' you. I had another guest I had to get breakfast for. What would you like to drink? I've got coffee, orange juice, apple juice, milk, all of the above if you like."

"Coffee and orange juice," I said.

She walked back to the kitchen while I sat down at the table, which was set with a poinsettia print tablecloth and Christmas place settings trimmed in red and gold with holly leaf decorations. The centerpiece was a glass chimney and candle set in a holly wreath.

A few minutes later Dawna returned to the dining room holding a casserole dish and a silver serving spoon. "My festive breakfast casserole is one of our guests' favorites," she said. "It has pork sausage, cheddar, picante sauce, bread, and eggs. It's delicious."

"It looks good," I said.

"It is." She spooned a large serving of casserole onto my plate, then said, "Oh, I forgot your beverages."

She went back to the kitchen, returning a minute later with my juice and coffee. She set the drinks down and sat down across the table from me, presumably to watch me eat.

I took a couple of bites, expecting her to say something, but she didn't. She just sat there watching me, which, frankly, was a little uncomfortable. Finally I asked, "How's business?"

She sighed. "A little slow but it's picking up. It's not tourist season yet. During Sturgis we just rent the whole place out. You know what Sturgis is?"

I nodded. "I had employees who went every year. The stories they would tell . . ."

"Oh yes, there are stories. Last year there was a woman on a Harley who called herself 'Lady Godiva.' I don't need to tell you what she was wearing. Or not wearing."

The town of Sturgis, South Dakota, is the epicenter of the world's largest annual gathering of Harley-Davidson motorcycle riders. Every August, thousands of bikers, from business magnates to Hells Angels, descend on the town. There's nothing else like it in the world.

"How far are we from Sturgis?" I asked.

"A little over fifty miles."

"I'd like to see that sometime."

"There's not much to see this time of year," she said. "'Course it's not as wild as it used to be. It's like Christmas—it got commercialized."

Just then I heard a doorknob turn and the back door opened. I looked over as Dawna's other guest entered the room. It was Pamela.

"Hi, Alan," she said softly.

I stared at her in disbelief. "I thought you'd given up."

"No."

I looked at her for a moment then stood. "Fine. Follow me to Key West if you want. But you should get some better shoes." I turned to Dawna, whose eyes were nervously darting back and forth between us. "I need my bill."

"I'll get it," she said, standing quickly. She walked over

to her cubbyholed maple desk. "It will be eighty-nine dollars for the night." She held up a handwritten invoice. "Ninety-two fifty-six with tax."

Pamela stared at me. "Alan . . . Just five minutes. Please."

"I told you no."

I handed Dawna my credit card, then, as it was processing, went back to my room and got my backpack. When I returned to the dining room, Pamela was still there. I retrieved my credit card, signed the bill, then walked past Pamela to the front door.

"Please, just hear me out," she said.

"I told you yesterday, we have nothing to talk about. Nothing's changed since then." I walked out the door, slamming it shut behind me.

As I reached the other end of the parking lot, Pamela stepped outside. "You owe me," she shouted.

I spun around. "What?"

"You owe me."

A flash of rage engulfed me. "I owe *you?*"

She walked halfway across the parking lot to me. "Yes. You do."

"For what? For abandoning a little girl? For ruining my wife's life?"

She looked me in the eyes. "Her life wasn't ruined. She had you." She stepped closer, and her voice was calmer. "If I hadn't been a bad mother, would McKale have been yours the way she was? Would she have needed you like she did? Would she have even married you?"

Her questions took me aback. After a moment I said, "Go home, Pamela. Go back to wherever you've been hiding all these years. You had your chance."

Her eyes welled up with tears.

I turned back to the road. I walked fifty yards or so

before I glanced back. I couldn't believe it. She was still following me. Though, this time, with a slight limp. It didn't take me long to leave her far behind.

The strangest thing I saw that morning—other than Pamela—was a sign for *Red Ass Rhubarb Wine*. If I hadn't been in such a hurry to flee my pursuer I might have stopped for a taste. I could have used some wine. Pamela's questions bothered me.

Just outside Hill City I came to a place called Mistletoe Ranch, which wasn't really a ranch, but a Christmas emporium. A sign in front of the building proclaimed it *The Ultimate Christmas Store*.

McKale was a die-hard fan of Christmas and, as she had in so many of her passions, converted me as well. Even in spring I couldn't resist the allure of the season. Since I hadn't seen Pamela for more than an hour I went inside.

The place was indeed full of Christmas. Tinny, banjo Christmas music played from overhead speakers, and the room smelled of pine and buttercream scented candles. The walls were shelved and piled high with hundreds of unique holiday decorations, knickknacks, and collectibles, from Betty Boop Christmas ornaments to Elvis stockings to miniature porcelain Christmas villages.

There were a few things I wanted but since purchasing anything I'd have to carry would have been absurd (although I did consider purchasing a Marilyn Monroe ornament to hang from the back of my pack) I left empty-handed. My stop wasn't a waste of time, though. The visit had distracted me from the emotions stirred up by my encounter with Pamela. Whatever the season, a healthy dose of Christmas lifts the spirits.

As I opened the door to leave I looked both ways to see if Pamela was there. She was. I don't know how she knew I had gone into the store—she was nowhere in sight when I'd gone in—but she was there, standing across the road waiting for me.

I started off again, walking even faster than usual. Within fifteen minutes Pamela was out of sight, though by now I no longer assumed that she'd given up her quest.

A few miles past Hill City, the highway split. I continued on 16 east until it ran north again. Around noon I reached the historic Rockerville Café, where I stopped to eat a hamburger and failed to learn what made the place historic. Actually, I didn't care what made the place historic. After traveling through Idaho, where everything was historic, the label had lost its luster.

I didn't stay long. I hoped I had lost Pamela where the highway split, but in case I hadn't, I didn't want to give her the chance to catch up. I was relieved she wasn't standing there as I left the café.

A couple miles from the café a Forest Service sign informed me that I was leaving the Black Hills National Forest, though you wouldn't know it by looking; as far as I could see, the road continued to be lined with forest, as well as tourist attractions, hoping to catch the crumbs from Mount Rushmore's table.

I passed another Christmas shop (apparently Christmas is a moneymaker in South Dakota) and Bear Country USA—a 250-acre drive-through wildlife park, boasting the world's largest collection of privately owned black bears. I could see some of the bears from the highway and I thought back to the grizzly I had encountered in the wild three weeks earlier in Yellowstone. These captive bears didn't look nearly as lively or dangerous. In fact, they looked sedated and about as frisky as my father an hour after Thanksgiving dinner.

There were more tourist attractions in this stretch than perhaps anywhere else in America. I passed a reptile zoo, a wax museum, a corn maze, and a mountain zip line, the latter of which reminded me of my eleventh birthday.

That was a birthday to remember. Actually, it was impossible to forget. My dad, in a rare moment of introspection, decided that in the absence of a mother, a dutiful father should probably throw his only son a birthday party at least once in his life. This was something that he'd never done before, so, not surprisingly, he was clueless. I once saw my dad dismantle a five-horsepower Briggs & Stratton engine from our lawn mower, strip it down to its block, then reassemble it perfectly. But he couldn't put a birthday party together to save his life.

He started by inviting random children from the neighborhood, many of whom I didn't know, including two sisters whose family had just migrated to the U.S. from Hungary. The girls didn't speak English, or at least not that any of us had heard, and they huddled together the whole time speaking in frightened whispers to each other.

My father borrowed a minivan and took all seven of us to a Pizza Hut (which wasn't a bad call), then to a zip line he'd found a coupon for, located about forty-five minutes from our home.

The Hungarian girls only became relevant to the party when the younger of the girls (none of us ever learned either of their names) somehow got her long blond hair caught in the pulley, stopping her mid-ride and leaving her dangling hundreds of feet above the ground, screaming hysterically.

The rescue mission was well worth the price of admission. We, and a few dozen others from waiting groups, gaped as one of the zip line workers donned thick gloves and shimmied down the line until he was close enough to cut the girl's hair with a pair of wire cutters, sending her rolling down the line. We clapped and hooted when she was free, unanimously judging the rescue operation a great success. All of us, that is, but the sisters, who apparently thought otherwise, evidenced by their red and tear-stained faces. The older girl kept examining her sister's chopped hair and crying.

When we got back to our neighborhood, my dad dropped the sisters off in their driveway and sped away before they got to their door. I asked if he should tell their parents what had happened, but my dad just mumbled something like, "They don't speak English that well," and "They're from a communist-bloc country, they're used to things like that." I pondered that statement for years, and every time I heard something about a communist country, I imagined unhappy girls with erratically lopped off tufts of hair.

By twilight I was close to Rapid City and had I been in a car I would have driven on to the city center, but I had already walked twenty miles and there was an ominously steep hill looming ahead of me, so I ended my day outside the city limits at the Happy Holiday Motel. I expected at any moment to see Pamela step out of a car behind me but she never did. I was foolishly optimistic that she had finally given up and gone home. I was wrong.

CHAPTER

Five

Last night I dreamt I was kissing McKale.
As I pressed my lips against hers I was
filled with the most exquisite joy. Then
my joy turned to horror when I realized
that I wasn't kissing her, but giving
her mouth-to-mouth resuscitation.

Alan Christoffersen's diary

I woke the next morning wondering what Pamela wanted to say. If she had come to apologize, she was too late for that. The person she needed to apologize to was already gone.

After breakfast, I stretched my legs and back, then donned my pack and started walking.

I don't like days that start with large hills; the same was figuratively true when I ran an advertising agency. In less than two hours, Rapid City loomed ahead of me.

Rapid City reminded me a lot of Spokane. Since it was the first city of any real size I'd walked through since Cody, Wyoming, I decided to bypass the truck route and walk through town. No doubt inspired by Mount Rushmore's presidential fervor, there was a bronze statue on every street corner depicting a U.S. president engaged in some activity demonstrative of their term in office.

I didn't recognize many of them. Actually, most of them. This wasn't surprising. I mean, could anyone alive today pick James K. Polk from a police lineup or recognize Rutherford B. Hayes if they bumped into him in an elevator? Or what about William Henry Harrison, our shortest-lived president, who died just thirty-two days into office? I wondered what his statue looked like—a man in bed?

At the end of the strip, I turned left on East Boulevard to I-90. Walking in the city is always slower, and adding to my delay was some major road construction that forced me to dodge road maintenance workers and machinery for the next few miles. Not halfway through the city I was longing for the wilds again.

The only restaurant I encountered, other than the usual fast-food chains, was a Vietnamese restaurant, which sounded interesting. Once inside, though, I ended up ordering things that weren't Vietnamese—sesame chicken and Thai curry shrimp. They both were good. I ate quickly, eager to get back on my way and out of the city.

I stopped at a grocery store to stock up on rations: canned fruit, beef jerky, Clif Bars, bread, Pop-Tarts, a jar of artichoke hearts, and water. A half hour past the grocery store I reached Interstate 90 and headed east.

The interstate was dangerously busy, and most of the way I was forced to walk on the freeway's uneven, cratered shoulder.

By late afternoon the traffic eased as the landscape turned dull and barren. Acres of trailer parks and the lack of trees rendered the scenery drab. I felt like I was in eastern Wyoming again. That is until I saw my first Wall Drug sign.

Wall Drug is a legend, a true American success story and a case study in the power of advertising. Any adman worth his salt knows about Wall Drug.

The Wall Drug story began in 1931, when Ted Hustead, a young pharmacist working in Canova, South Dakota, made the fateful decision to strike out on his own. With a three-thousand-dollar inheritance from his father, he and his wife, Dorothy, hopped in their Model T and began scouring the state for a store to purchase.

Their search led them to the small, desolate town of Wall, South Dakota—an area of the state Ted's father-in-law described as "about as Godforsaken as you can get." The town was not only in the middle of nowhere, but it was poor as well—the residents were mostly the impoverished survivors of the Great Depression. Wall was hardly the kind of place to start a successful business.

In spite of the obvious drawbacks, Ted and Dorothy

felt at home in the small town, largely due to the fact that it had a Catholic church where they could go to Mass every day. They prayed about their decision and, feeling divine guidance, decided to buy the struggling drugstore.

As the months, then years, passed, their drugstore floundered, constantly teetering on the brink of failure. In spite of his faith, Ted began to wonder if they'd done the right thing. He finally decided to give the store five more years. "Five good years," he told his wife, "and if it doesn't work by then . . ."

Dorothy was more optimistic. "In a few years Mount Rushmore will be finished," she reasoned. "There will be a lot more traffic and business."

She was half right. Every year the traffic that passed by Wall increased, but their business didn't. Day after day the couple sat on the porch of their store and watched the cars drive by—few of them stopping in the dusty town.

Then, one day, Dorothy had an epiphany. Being in the middle of nowhere meant that all those people passing them by had been driving a long time across the hot, desolate prairie. "They're thirsty," Dorothy said. "They want water. Ice-cold water. And we've got plenty of ice and plenty of water."

The next day, Ted painted several signs offering FREE ICE WATER. Then, following the model of the famous Burma Shave highway signs, he planted his signs every mile or so leading to their store. By the time he got back to their drugstore, people had already begun stopping for free ice water and Dorothy was running around like crazy trying to keep up with their other purchases.

Today, the world-famous drugstore draws millions of

visitors a year, up to twenty thousand visitors a day. Their advertising signs, like the one I'd just seen, were smaller than conventional billboards, but what they lacked in size they made up for in frequency, with appeals designed to reach everyone.

From the moment I saw that first sign, there was always a sign in view.

Get a Milkshake. Wall Drug

Get a Rootbeer. Wall Drug

Pretty Near. Wall Drug

Free Coffee & Donuts for Vietnam Vets. Wall Drug

Still a slave to an old advertising habit of mine, I took out my journal and began writing down the slogans. When I started my recording, I had already passed four signs and I was still more than forty miles from Wall.

By evening I had put in around nineteen miles through vast stretches of nothing but plains, fields, and Wall Drug signage. The last of the day's light was beginning to fade, and I was looking for a place to camp when a car pulled up about fifty feet behind me. The door opened and Pamela got out. She thanked the driver, then shut the door.

"Alan," she said.

Unbelievable, I thought. *She's the Energizer Bunny of stalkers.*

I postponed my plan to camp and continued to walk. Pamela followed. I walked perhaps another five miles until there was no sign of her—or anything else—except a lot of nothing and the Wall Drug signs. It was a warm night and I rolled out my pad and sleeping bag under a freeway overpass. I wondered how Pamela was planning to spend the night.

The next morning I woke a little before sunrise. I looked around for Pamela but didn't see her, though I was certain she was out there somewhere. I wondered how she was surviving. She had no provisions, no sleeping bag, no air mattress, just a simple ladies' handbag and bad shoes. *Had she really slept on the road?*

I ate two Pop-Tarts, a Clif Bar, and an apple, then set off for a new day of Wall Drug signs.

Wall Drug. Historical Photos

Wall Drug. 33 Miles to Go

All Roads Lead to Wall Drug

Western Wear. Wall Drug

Road Trip. Wall Drug

Sheriff on Duty. Wall Drug

Western Home Décor. Wall Drug

Wall Drug or Bust

6 foot Rabbit. Wall Drug

Buffalo Burgers. Wall Drug

Free Ice Water. Wall Drug

Be Yourself. Wall Drug

Badlands Maps. Wall Drug

Frosted Mug Beer. Wall Drug

Dig it. Wall Drug

After an hour of walking, I made out the figure of someone walking ahead of me in the distance. *Couldn't be*, I thought. *Couldn't be her.*

It was. Pamela was walking in front of me. Even from a distance I could see that her limping had increased.

I crossed to the opposite side of the road. When I was adjacent to her I could see how bad she looked. Her hair was matted and she looked pale.

"Please talk to me," she said. "I'm begging."

"Go home, Pamela."

"I'm not quitting," she said. "I don't care if it kills me."

"It might," I said.

"Please."

I kept on walking.

Wall Drug USA exit 110

Wall Drug Since 1931

Coffee 5 cents. Wall Drug

A Dakota Must See. Wall Drug

Refreshing Free Ice Water. Wall Drug

Around noon I stopped along the side of the road to eat a can of fruit cocktail, another Clif Bar, and my own invention, a beef jerky sandwich. The land was flat but with the exception of the signs, there was nothing as far as the eye could see, including Pamela.

Tourist Info. Wall Drug

Skinny Saloon. Wall Drug

It's cool. Wall Drug

Experience Wall Drug Mining Co.

American Icon. Wall Drug

Kids Love Wall Drug

As I walked through the unvarying scenery my mind wandered. I wondered how Kailamai and Nicole were doing. Nicole was the woman who had taken me in after I was attacked near Spokane. Kailamai was a young runaway I had met shortly after near Coeur d'Alene, Idaho. I had introduced them to each other, and Kailamai was now Nicole's roommate. It felt like months since I'd seen them. I counted back the days. Thirty-six days. Just thirty-six days. It felt like six months. At least.

I remembered that back in Spokane I had promised to

call my father every week. He had bought me a phone for that express purpose. I wasn't sure whether I would have reception or not, but I stopped, took my cell phone from my pack, and turned it on. There were two bars. I held down on the number 1, calling my father. He answered before the second ring.

"Where are you?" he asked.

"Nowhere. I'm in South Dakota on Highway 90."

"Did you pass Wall Drug yet?" he asked.

"You know about Wall Drug?" I asked.

"Everyone knows about Wall Drug," he said. "It was in *Reader's Digest* and *Life* magazine." In my father's world, *everyone* had read those magazines. Still did.

"No. But I've passed a bunch of their signs."

"They're famous for those signs. How are you?"

"I'm doing okay. And you?"

"You know me. Nothing changes."

"Have you heard from Nicole?"

"Yes. We talk a couple times a week. She's really a pleasant young lady. We're taking things slowly. I got her into an IRA and some mutual funds."

"How is she?" I asked.

"She's doing great. She got that inheritance."

"I didn't mean financially," I said.

"Oh. Well I wouldn't know about that. She sounded well."

"Did she mention Kailamai?"

"Who?"

"I guess not."

"She asked about you. She wanted to know if I'd heard from you and how you're doing."

"Tell her I'm still walking."

He laughed. "I'll do that. If I didn't know better, I'd say she sounds a little smitten."

"With who?"

"Who do you think?"

I wasn't sure how to respond so I changed the subject. "Something weird is happening. McKale's mother . . ."

"Pamela," my father said. I was surprised he knew her name. But of course he did. He and Sam had been neighbors for more than a decade.

"Right. Pamela," I said. "She's following me."

"Following you? In her car?"

"On foot."

"She's walking with you?"

"Not with me. She's following me."

There was a long pause. "What does she want?"

"I'm not sure. She says she wants to talk to me."

"About what?"

"No idea."

"Why don't you ask her?"

"I'm trying to avoid her."

"I saw her at McKale's funeral," he said.

"I know. So did I."

"Maybe you should just find out what she wants."

"Maybe she should just go home," I said.

He didn't say anything. After a moment I said, "Remember that time you threw me that birthday party and we went to the zip line?"

"Yes. And that German girl got her hair stuck in the pulley."

"She was Hungarian."

"That's right. What about it?"

"Thanks," I said.

"For what?"

"For throwing me the party."

He was quiet for a moment. "You're welcome."

"I'll talk to you next week," I said.

"Okay. Be safe."

"Bye."

I hung up the phone, stowed it in my pack, and kept walking.

Homemade Pie. Wall Drug

Fast Food. Wall Drug

Homemade Ice Cream. Wall Drug

Wall Drug as seen on CMT

5 cents Hot Coffee. Wall Drug

Western Wear. Wall Drug

Something to Crow About. Wall Drug

Homemade Donuts. Wall Drug

Free Coffee and Donuts for Honeymooners

That night I slept behind one of the Wall Drug signs—an advertisement for five-cent coffee. The road was flat and smooth, which made walking easy, but there were no services. Ted Hustead's father-in-law was right, this place was as "Godforsaken" as you'll find on the planet. Fortunately I was prepared. I had asked about this stretch at the grocery store back in Rapid City and was told that there was nothing until Wall. I had packed several liters of water, which, in spite of the weight, I drank sparingly.

This led me to wonder: where was Pamela getting water?

CHAPTER

Six

My stalker has forced my hand.

Alan Christoffersen's diary

I didn't sleep well that night. The ground felt harder than usual, if that was possible. My water was warm and free ice water at Wall Drug was sounding pretty good. Dorothy Hustead was a smart lady.

At breakfast I noticed that a field mouse had gotten into my pack and chewed off the corner of a peanut butter Clif Bar. I broke off the spoiled corner, then ate the rest of the bar, along with some bread and my last can of fruit cocktail. I packed up my sleeping bag then started off, my back aching a little. I was ready for a real bed.

After two miles the landscape opened to a valley—a welcome relief from the tedium of endless plains. The signs were still there.

New Dinosaur. Wall Drug

Camping Supplies. Wall Drug

Great Hot Coffee 5 Cents. Wall Drug

After such a psychological assault, could anyone possibly not stop at Wall Drug? This was clearly an instance where, like the California Raisins or Pepto-Bismol, the advertising became greater than the product.

After five miles I passed the town of Wasta. Strange name. I have no idea what it means.

Wasta wasn't much of a town, really, but it was the first I'd seen since Rapid City. The highway crossed the Cheyenne River, which was the first body of water I'd seen in a while. A half hour past the river, I came to a rest area, where I stopped to use the bathroom. I took some extra toilet paper because I was running low. I filled up my water bottles with fresh water.

As I strapped the bottles to my waistband, the thought returned to me, what was Pamela doing for water? What if she really meant what she'd said about dying? I hoped, for her sake, that she'd gotten smart and caught a ride back to Custer, or wherever she'd left her car. She had to have. She couldn't have made it this far without finding water somewhere.

After my stop at the rest area, the frequency of the Wall Drug assault increased, assuring me that I was getting close. At my current pace, I would reach Wall by late afternoon.

Black Hills Gold. Wall Drug

Exit 109. Wall Drug

Experience Wall Drug

Coffee 5 cents. Wall Drug

Conoco and Wall Drug

The Wild West. Wall Drug

Tour Bus Stop. Wall Drug

Free Coffee and Donuts for Veterans. Wall Drug

Famous Western Art Gallery——A Wall Drug Must See

I was still keeping track of the signs in my journal. Out of curiosity, I counted the entries when I stopped for lunch. Fifty-two. And that was just what I'd passed going east. I was sure there were just as many on the other side of Wall. That was more than a hundred signs. Considering where the signs were placed, on the outskirts of farms, I figured that the Wall Drug folk weren't paying usual advertising rates, as an outdoor campaign of that magnitude would cost a fortune. It was probably handled as a neighbor deal, a weekly pie or two, or free ice cream for the farmer's kids. Southern South Dakota still seemed to be that kind of place.

A couple of miles later, I saw train tracks on the south side of the road. I wondered where they had been for the last fifty miles.

An hour after lunch I came upon a decent-sized pond with inviting blue water. I climbed down the sloped shoulder of the highway to the edge of the pond. When there were no cars in sight, I stripped down and jumped in. I hadn't bathed for two days, not since the Happy Holiday Motel, and I was as sticky as a roll of flypaper. The water felt magnificent. I washed my hair and body with a small bottle of shampoo I had left over from the Holly House Bed and Breakfast.

I bathed for about twenty minutes, dried myself off, dressed, and climbed back to the highway. I had been walking for two hours when I heard the familiar sound of a car stopping behind me. Pamela. *At least she doesn't have any trouble getting people to pick her up,* I thought. Of course, if I saw a stranger—a mature woman—hitchhiking along this road, my conscience wouldn't let me pass her by. But to me she was no stranger. I knew what she had done.

As I watched her climb out of the car, I could tell that something was wrong. The driver of the car was saying something to her; his words, though indistinguishable, sounded pleading. Pamela offered a curt "thank you" and shut the car door, staggering a little as she stepped back. Even from a distance I could see that she wasn't okay. She was leaning to one side and her steps were awkward.

I had once read about people crawling to Mecca to atone for their sins. I wondered if, on some level, Pamela saw this journey as her penance. Maybe she really was willing to walk herself to death. I didn't want to think about it. I continued on past two more signs.

Wall Drug, USA. Just Ahead

Homemade Lunch Specials. Wall Drug

A few minutes later I looked back. Pamela was farther behind than I thought she would be. Actually, it looked like she hadn't taken more than a few steps since she'd left the car. I continued walking but turned back less than a minute later. Pamela was facedown on the ground.

I dropped my pack on the side of the road and started jogging back to her.

As I neared her I grew more anxious. She wasn't moving. When I was maybe a hundred feet away I cupped my hands to my mouth and shouted, "Pamela!"

Nothing. I shouted again, "Pamela!"

She slowly raised her head so that her chin touched the asphalt. She looked at me with a confused expression. When I reached her, I crouched down next to her. "Are you okay?"

She didn't answer. Her eyes darted quickly back and forth. Her face was scraped on one side, and her skin was bright red. Her lips were cracked. Her mouth was moving but she was having trouble speaking. "I'm sorry," she said.

"When was the last time you had something to drink?" I asked, taking a water bottle from my waist belt.

"Long time," she said, her words slurred.

I held the bottle up to her lips. She opened her mouth and I squirted the water inside. She gulped heavily, though much of it ran down the side of her mouth and face. She stopped drinking only a few times and drained the bottle in less than a minute. When the bottle was empty she lay forward again, her face in her arms.

She lay there for another fifteen minutes before she rolled to her side. "Thank you."

"Would you like some more water?"

She nodded. "Yes." Her speech already sounded better.

I brought out my other bottle, which was only half full. She held it herself this time and quickly drained it. When she'd finished the water I handed her a Clif Bar from my pants pocket. "Here, have this," I said, peeling back the wrapper. "You need some carbs."

She ate the bar quickly.

"That was stupid following me," I said. "You're not prepared for this. You could have died out here."

She slowly looked up at me. "Would it have mattered?"

I looked at her for a long time then said, "There's a hotel in Wall. Let's get you there. Can you walk?"

"Will you talk to me if I do?"

"No," I said.

"Then go," she said. "Just leave me."

"I'm not leaving you."

In spite of her weakness, she shouted, "Leave me!" She lay her face back down on the asphalt. "Just leave me."

I looked around. There was no one in sight. I breathed out slowly. "Okay. I'll talk to you."

She looked up at me doubtfully.

"Come on," I said. "I mean it. Come with me to Wall and we'll talk."

She closed her eyes for a moment, then slowly struggled up to her knees. I took her arm and helped her to her feet. The front of her blouse was dirty and her arms were red and pocked from the rocks she had fallen on.

She took a step, leaning heavily against me. Then another. It took us more than twenty minutes to get back to my pack and nearly forty-five minutes to walk the mile to the Wall off-ramp. Only a few cars passed us, and even though I put my thumb out, none of them stopped. We passed three more signs on the way.

Wall Drug Exit

Wall Drug Keep Left. Free Mainstreet Parking

Wall Drug Straight Ahead, 4 blocks

Pamela was staggering and breathing heavily at the top of the highway off-ramp. "May I rest a moment?"

"Of course," I said. I led her to the curved, aluminum surface of the guardrail where she sat.

I stepped back to the edge of the road and stuck out my thumb when I saw an approaching vehicle, which immediately slowed—a phenomenon not uncommon in small towns. The gray-haired man driving an old truck pulled off the road slightly past us. I walked up to the truck's window as it rolled down. The man reached over and turned off his radio that had been blaring country music then looked out at me. "Need a lift?"

"Yes. Just into town."

"It's only a half mile. Hop in front."

I walked back and helped Pamela to the truck, practically pushing her up into the cab and onto the bench seat. Then I threw my pack into the truck's bed and climbed into the cab next to Pamela.

"How are you all this afternoon?" the man asked.

Pamela forced a smile. "Thank you for stopping."

"My pleasure," he said.

"We're just going to the first hotel," I said to the man.

"That'd be Ann's," he replied. "Right next to Wall Drug." He signaled, checked his mirror, then drove into town.

Ann's Motel was a small inn on Wall's main drag, west of the Wall Drug complex. The man pulled into the motel's parking lot and stopped his truck in front of the lobby door. I got out, then helped Pamela, holding her arm as she stepped down.

"Thanks," I said to the man.

"Don't mention it. Don't forget your pack."

Pamela said, "Thank you, sir."

"My pleasure, ma'am," he said kindly.

I shut the door after Pamela and grabbed my pack from the truck's bed. I slapped the back of the truck and the truck rattled off.

Pamela limped over to a wood bench near the motel lobby while I went inside to check on rooms. Fortunately, the motel had vacancies and I got two rooms on the street level. There was a small, glass-door refrigerator in the lobby with beverages for sale and I bought a bottle of Gatorade. I got our keys from the clerk, then went back out to Pamela. I handed her a key and the Gatorade. "You should drink that right away. It will help."

"Thank you," she said, stowing the bottle in her bag.

"I got you a room on the main floor. One-eleven, right over there."

Pamela stood on her own, her bag around her shoulder. "May we talk now?"

"Not yet," I said. "I want you to drink that and get some rest. I'll go see what they have to eat over at the drugstore then we'll go to dinner later. We'll talk then."

"Thank you," she said. "Thank you."

"Don't thank me. You gave me no choice."

"We always have a choice," she said.

In light of the circumstances of our relationship I found her comment intriguing. I helped her to her room, then went to my own.

My room was a small rectangle, furnished with two full beds with stiff mattresses and aged floral pattern comforters. After so many days without amenities, it was as welcome to me as a suite at the Four Seasons.

I leaned my pack against the wall and flopped onto the bed. I wondered what could be so important for Pamela to say that she had risked her life to follow me. What could she possibly have to say in her own defense? Most of all, I wondered what McKale would have made of it all.

I remember the first time I asked McKale where her mother was. I was only nine years old and had lost my own mother less than a year earlier, so the topic of mothers was one of interest to me. Especially missing ones.

"We kicked her out," McKale said.

I looked at her in amazement. "Why did you do that?"

"Me and my dad don't want her anymore. We even threw away all her pictures so we don't have to look at her."

Her answer was the strangest thing I had ever heard. Even at that age I guessed there was more to her story, but I also knew better than to ask.

A week later we were in McKale's backyard climbing an

avocado tree when a piece of paper fell out of her pants pocket. I jumped down and picked it up, then unfolded it. It was a creased photograph of a woman.

"Who's this?" I asked, holding the picture up.

McKale looked horrified. "It's no one."

"It's someone," I said.

McKale climbed down from the tree. "If you must know, it's my mom."

"I thought you said you threw away all her pictures," I said, naïvely pleased to have caught McKale in a lie.

Her eyes welled up with tears. "You are so dumb," she said. She ran into her house leaving me alone in her backyard holding the picture of Pamela and wondering what I'd done wrong.

With that memory replaying in my mind, I closed my eyes and fell asleep.

CHAPTER

Seven

Once you have opened the book
to another's life, the cover
never looks the same.

Alan Christoffersen's Diary

I woke with a start. I hadn't intended to fall asleep, but after three nights of sleeping on hard ground, I was out before I knew it. I looked at the clock and saw that it was almost a quarter to nine. I groaned. "Pamela."

I went to the bathroom and washed my face, then went outside and knocked on Pamela's door. She answered immediately. "I wondered if you'd changed your mind."

"No. Sorry, I fell asleep. Are you ready?"

She had probably been waiting for several hours, but she only nodded. "I'm ready." She stepped out, shutting the door behind her. "Thank you."

Wall Drug is not the single store it started as—it's now a long row of buildings that look like a cross between a strip mall and a movie studio's back lot western town. Wall Drug's restaurant was located near the middle of the complex.

I held the door for Pamela as we walked into a large dining room separated into two eating areas by an open kitchen and a long row of cafeteria-style tray rails.

The seating area closest to the street had an ice cream bar and pastry counter with pie, brownies, and other confections, including a platter of their famous "free for veterans" cake doughnuts.

The wood-panel walls were hung with cowboy art: paintings of cowboys, horses, and Native Americans. They were all for sale, which was true of pretty much everything in the building.

There was only one couple in the dining room. Pamela followed me over to a table in the southwest corner of the room—opposite the other diners.

"We can sit here," I said. "What do you want to eat?"

"Whatever you get is fine," Pamela replied.

After looking over the hand-scrawled menu board, I ordered a couple of Cokes, two cups of chicken noodle soup, and French dip sandwiches. I paid for the meal and went back to the table where Pamela was sitting quietly. For a moment we just looked at each other, then I clasped my hands on the table in front of me. "What did you want to talk about?"

Pamela took a deep breath. "I'm not sure where to begin."

After a moment I said, "Why don't you begin by telling me why you abandoned your daughter?" My words sounded harsher than I had intended.

She nodded. "All right." She looked down for a long time. When she looked back up at me, her eyes had a dark sadness to them. "I want you to understand something. What I'm going to tell you isn't an excuse. It's a reason. If I could do things differently, I would." She looked into my eyes to see if I understood.

"Okay," I said.

She settled a little into her chair. "I should start at the beginning." She took another deep breath. "I was too young when I married Sam. I was only eighteen. Way too young. My life at home was so terrible, and I suppose I was just looking for a way to get out. My parents were always fighting. They were always screaming and shouting at each other. Sometimes their fights would turn violent. Once the neighbors called the police, but when they arrived, my parents just yelled at them. The police left shaking their heads. It was madness."

"Were they ever violent with you?" I asked.

"My mother hit me a few times. But seeing them hurt each other was worse. I used to hide in my closet with my hands over my ears so I wouldn't hear them. But of course I heard every word. I always thought it was my fault. I know that's not rational, but children aren't terribly rational.

"This pattern went on my whole childhood. I don't know why they didn't get counseling or just leave each other. They were just sick, I guess. Or their relationship was. It was their cycle. But I never got used to it.

"When I was old enough, I got a job waitressing at a pancake house. I worked as much as I could, and when I wasn't working I'd hang out with my friends. We would stay out really late, and I would sleep over at their houses. For months I barely went home. I hadn't really run away from home, I just stopped going there.

"The first time I went home after I'd been away for more than a week, I thought my parents would be upset and worried about me. But it was more like I had never been gone. My father wasn't there, and my mom didn't even ask where I'd been.

"Once I graduated from high school, I stopped going home at all. I spent most of my time with one of the other waitresses at the restaurant. Her name was Claire. She was a friend from school and had helped get me the job in the first place. We'd work until closing, then we'd go out to parties, then sleep at her place. Eventually I just moved in with her.

"That's where I met Sam. He was Claire's cousin. Sam was a lot older than me. Eight years older." She shook her head. "He was only twenty-six, but he seemed so old back then. I guess compared to me, he was. I had only known him a few weeks when he asked me out.

"He was different than the boys I'd been hanging out with. They were still kids. Sam was older. More mature.

On our third date, he asked me to marry him. I said yes. I wasn't sure if it was right, but it's like they say—a drowning person isn't picky about which lifeboat she climbs into. I wasn't really sure about anything at the time except that I liked him. And if I was going to get married, I thought that marrying someone older would be safer.

"I didn't know until two days before our wedding that Sam had already been married once before. I guess his ex was a pretty strong-willed woman, and he couldn't take it, so he had the marriage annulled six weeks after their wedding. I found out later that he'd told Claire that his next wife would be someone younger. Someone who would obey him. I guess that's why he married me. I was pretty submissive. I did whatever he told me to do.

"So we got married. Our wedding day was the happiest day of my life. I was so hopeful. Then, on our honeymoon, Sam told me to stop using birth control. He said he wanted a baby right away. He didn't so much tell me he wanted one, as he demanded one—as if my feelings on the matter were irrelevant. We had never even discussed children before then. I told him that I didn't think I was old enough to have a baby. I still felt like a kid myself. The truth is, I didn't even know if I wanted one. I didn't want anyone to have to live a life like mine.

"But Sam was older than me and he said he didn't want to be an old man when his kids were in high school. I knew in my heart that I wasn't ready. But Sam didn't care what I thought. He had this stupid line he'd heard somewhere— 'they're not your feelings, they're your failings.' He just got meaner every time I refused. We started fighting about it almost all the time. I couldn't stand it. It was like we had become my parents.

"Then everything came to a climax. After months of

fighting, Sam gave me an ultimatum. He said if I wouldn't have his baby, he would find someone who would. He gave me until his birthday to make up my mind."

As Pamela spoke I realized that in spite of all the times I'd seen McKale's father, I really didn't know him. To me he was a laid-back, easygoing guy, who worked a lot and listened to vinyl records when he wasn't working, which was partially why McKale had always been with me. I wasn't sure that I believed everything that Pamela was saying, but it was clear to me that she did.

"Sam said that he would leave you?" I asked.

Pamela's eyes teared up. She nodded. "More than once. I was devastated. I don't even think it was about the baby anymore; it was about controlling me. He was good at punishing me. At first he was passive-aggressive. He would go days without speaking to me. I was always more needy than him, so after a day I would be begging him to talk to me—to love me. Then he began treating me like a child. One night he said he was going to spank me. I thought he was joking. But he wasn't. He made me go over his knee and he spanked me until I cried. It was so humiliating. I felt like a child again."

Pamela suddenly started crying and I noticed that the diners at the other table were looking at us. I waited for Pamela to gain her composure. As we sat there, the counter bell rang. The woman at the counter said in a bright voice, "Your order's up."

Pamela was dabbing her eyes with a paper napkin. "I'll get that," I said. I walked up to the counter, got our tray, and brought it back to the table.

By the time I was seated, Pamela had settled some. "Do you want to eat or go on?" she asked.

"Go on," I said. "So why didn't you just leave him?"

"Would you have left your wife?" she asked.

"McKale wasn't abusive."

She shook her head. "I don't know why. I didn't really think of him as abusive. At least not then. To me, abuse was when you had bruises and broken bones, not just a broken heart." She looked at me. "I don't know. I guess you just have to go through it to understand. When people are in abusive situations, they measure things in contrasts. As much as Sam hurt me, leaving him would be even more painful. Besides, part of me always felt that I deserved to be treated poorly. It's what I knew. I was always trying to earn somebody's love.

"The thing is, I knew he would win. I knew, in the end, I would have to do what he said.

"I spent the next few days talking myself into it—telling myself what a good idea it was to have a baby and how great it would be to have a family. Or I'd tell myself, maybe once the baby came I'd feel differently, or what if I couldn't even get pregnant and all this pain was for nothing? I finally decided that giving in would be my birthday present to him.

"I knew that it was wrong—that I wasn't even close to being ready to be a mother. But there was nowhere else to go.

"On Sam's birthday I got up and made him breakfast and brought it out on a tray. Underneath his coffee cup I put a note that said, 'YES.'

"He looked up at me with this triumphant smile and said, 'Then let's get started.' "

Pamela was shaking her head. "Of course I got pregnant right away with McKale. I don't get it. People pray and beg God for a baby and never have one, and here I am hoping I won't get pregnant and I'm pregnant immediately.

"I was terrified. Sam just kept telling me that everything would be fine—that being a mother was a natural part of womanhood." Pamela grimaced. "As if he knew anything about being a woman." She looked into my eyes. "No matter what they say, it's not always a natural thing—at least not for everyone. After she was born I remember sitting in bed holding this beautiful little baby and thinking that I was supposed to be feeling something magical and wondering what was wrong with me. I never should have had a baby until I was ready. It wasn't fair to McKale. It wasn't fair to me."

Pamela wiped her eyes. "I felt insanely guilty that I didn't connect with her. Truthfully, I resented her. And I hated myself for resenting her.

"Of course, I couldn't tell Sam any of this. I tried once and he turned on me so fiercely, I was afraid he was going to hurt me." Growing up, I had seen Sam blow up a few times so I knew he was capable of extreme rage. "He told me that I was just selfish."

"What did you say to that?"

Pamela bowed her head a little. "I told him he was right."

Neither of us spoke for a while. She was spent, and I wasn't sure what to say. After a while she said, "Do you mind if I eat something?"

I realized that she probably hadn't eaten much for several days. "No. Of course not."

We both ate. Pamela wolfed down her sandwich, looking slightly embarrassed to be eating so quickly. When she'd finished the sandwich, she started on the soup, first with a spoon, then lifting the bowl. *She must have been starving*, I thought.

When she had finished everything she apologized. "I'm sorry. I haven't eaten for a while."

"No, I'm sorry, I should have let you eat. Would you like something else? Some pie?"

"No, thank you," she said. "Shall I continue?"

"Please," I said.

She looked down, collecting her thoughts. Her forehead furrowed. "Before I had McKale I was working as an office manager at a plumbing supply store. I had quit when McKale was born, but we struggled on just Sam's income, so when she started school, I went back to work.

"One day this really handsome man came in. Jeremy. He was a plumber but he could have been a model. I was having one of those really hard days when it was all I could do not to burst into tears. He asked if I was all right, and I started to cry. He was really sweet. He asked if I needed to talk to someone and offered to meet me after work for a coffee. I told him thank you, but I was married and he backed off.

"But it wasn't the last I saw of him. He became a regular customer and would come in several times a week. He would bring me a little box of chocolate cordials every time he came to sweeten my day. I began looking forward to his visits.

"One day Jeremy came in about lunchtime. As he waited for his order to be filled, we started in on our usual chat when he asked if I wanted to get something to eat. It was the right time, or wrong time, for him to ask. Sam and I had just had another big blowup that morning." Pamela paused and her voice softened. "I said yes.

"We ended up at his condo. It was only the beginning. We started meeting every week. Jeremy was single and had a great business, so he had a lot of money and was always buying me jewelry and clothes. I couldn't bring them home, not that Sam would have noticed. Sam was busy trying to get his insurance business off the ground so he worked late almost every night. He rarely called me during the day.

"After a year of our affair, Jeremy asked me to leave Sam and marry him. Sam and I had only grown more distant, so, honestly, Jeremy's proposal sounded great. Except there was one hitch. He said that he didn't want to be tied down to a kid. I understood that. I mean, I felt the same way. I had gotten married and pregnant so young that I'd never had the chance to see the world.

"I know it sounds awful." She looked into my eyes. "It *is* awful. I considered it. But I couldn't do it. McKale was only seven. I couldn't just leave her.

"Jeremy said he understood. He said that that was what he really loved about me, that I had a good heart—but he loved me so intensely, that if our relationship wasn't going anywhere, it would be best if we stopped seeing each other.

"He stopped calling me. He still came in to the store, but he wouldn't speak to me. It was agonizing. I was so in love with him. I wanted to be with him more than anything.

"At home, things with Sam just got worse. He never outright called me an awful mother, at least not then, but I knew he was thinking it. Maybe it was because I was thinking it.

"Then, one day, I went to pick McKale up from her babysitter and McKale said, 'I don't want to go home with you.' The babysitter was really embarrassed. She said, 'You don't mean that.' McKale said, 'Yes I do. I don't like her.' "

Pamela's eyes welled up again. "I know kids say dumb things, but it broke me. Sam hated me. Now McKale didn't want me. I cried all night. The next day I called Jeremy from work and begged him to take me back. I said I'd do whatever he wanted if he'd just take me back.

"He came and got me. I didn't go home after work. I just went straight to his place. I didn't even pick up McKale.

"Of course the babysitter was frantic. She called Sam to see if I'd been in an accident or something." Pamela wiped her eyes. "Or *something* . . . I got home that night after ten. McKale was in bed. Sam was waiting for me. He screamed at me for more than an hour. He said he had to cancel an important business meeting with a new client to pick up McKale. He told me that I was the most irresponsible mother on the planet—a horrible mother *and wife*.

"That was the final straw. I told him I was leaving. He said, 'You can't leave us.'

"I said, 'Yes, I can.' I went to our room, threw my things in a suitcase, and walked out to my car. Then I realized I hadn't even looked in on McKale. I desperately wanted to see her. But what would I say? Sam wouldn't have let me in anyway." Her eyes welled up with tears. "I never said good-bye." She wiped her eyes, then blew her nose into a paper napkin. "Jeremy and I were married a week after the divorce went through. We traveled. I told myself I was happy. But of course the marriage didn't work. When you have an affair with someone, the affair itself becomes the core of the relationship. The secret of the affair fuels the passion and the excitement. But once it's legitimized, it's just reality like everything else. Less than two years later, Jeremy cheated on me. I wasn't really surprised. It's like they say, 'If they'll do it *with* you, they'll do it *to* you.' "

Pamela sighed deeply. "Jeremy wasn't a good man. It

doesn't take a rocket scientist to figure that out, I mean, he was a cheater and he wanted me to leave my child. What more did I need to know? I guess I figured he was just like me."

"Did you ever consider going back to McKale?" I asked.

"All the time. For weeks I'd skip lunch so I could drive to McKale's school and watch her play at recess. I wanted to go back home, but the only way I could have gone back to Sam was on my knees. And he would have kept me there for the rest of my life. Maybe that's what I deserved, but I knew I couldn't do it. And what would that have taught my daughter?

"I eventually moved to Colorado to start a new life. But you can't run away from yourself. I married again in Colorado. That only lasted twenty-nine months. James. He left me too. He sent me an email to let me know he'd moved on." She laughed cynically. "I really know how to pick them, don't I?"

I frowned.

"After that, I grew hard. I convinced myself that real love doesn't exist and all men are pigs. But it was a lie. Real love does exist. You and McKale had it. It just didn't exist for me."

Pamela was quiet for a long time. Finally she said, "At least something good came out of my last marriage." She reached into her purse and brought out her cell phone. She pushed a key, then held the phone up for me to see. On the screen was a picture of a young lady maybe sixteen or seventeen years of age. She was pretty, with big brown eyes, long brown hair, and freckles. She looked a lot like McKale did at that age.

"McKale has a sister?" I asked.

Pamela nodded. "Her name is Hadley."

I took the phone and stared. "She looks just like her." I handed back the phone. "What was it like when she was born?"

"It was the way it should have been. The way it should have been for McKale."

"Was Hadley at the funeral?"

"No. She didn't even know about McKale. I thought it would be too confusing to her. But after the funeral, I told her."

"How did she respond?"

"She wasn't as surprised as I thought she'd be. She said she knew I had had another baby. I don't know how she knew that. But she thought I had given her up for adoption or aborted her. She was really upset that I hadn't told her about McKale. She had always wanted a sister."

"I can't believe McKale has a sister." At that moment there were a lot of different emotions swimming in my head, but anger wasn't one of them. My rage for her was gone—I just wasn't sure what had replaced it. Pity? Understanding? Maybe even sympathy. After a moment I said, "What do you want from me?"

She looked down at the table for a long time. When she finally looked up again her eyes were filled with tears. "Grace," she said softly.

"Grace?" I frowned. "Grace isn't mine to give. The one who needs to forgive you is gone."

"I just thought . . ." She exhaled. "When I saw you at the funeral . . . when I met you, I knew that you and McKale were one. I thought—I felt—that if you could find a way to forgive me then it would be the same as McKale forgiving me. And maybe I could find peace." She looked into my eyes. "And maybe you could too."

"What makes you think I don't have peace?" I asked.

"Because you can't hate and have peace."

I thought over her words. When I finally spoke I shook my head. "I don't know, Pamela."

She looked back down, closing her eyes to conceal her pain, though tears stole through the corners of her eyes. It pained me to add to all she'd been through.

After a moment I said, "This is just a lot to process. It's been a long day. I need to sleep on it."

She nodded understandingly. "We can go back to the motel."

I looked at her for a moment, then pushed my chair back from the table and stood. "Can I get you something else to eat? You could take it back to your room."

She shook her head as she stood. "No. I'm okay," she said softly.

We walked silently together back to the motel. I saw Pamela to her door. She inserted her room key, but instead of opening the door, turned to me. "Whatever you decide, thank you for listening. You have no idea how much it helps. Especially knowing that my girl found someone who truly loved her." She opened her door and stepped inside.

"Pamela."

She looked back at me.

"I'm sorry that you went through what you did."

She smiled sadly. "Thank you. Good night, Alan."

"Good night," I said.

She shut her door, and I went back to my room. I was emotionally exhausted. I just wanted to go to bed, but I hadn't washed my clothes in days and the motel had a tiny Laundromat. I gathered my clothes and put them in the washer, then went back to my room. I watched television until it was time to transfer my clothes to the dryer.

Then I returned to my room and the television. Finally, at eleven, I returned to the Laundromat and gathered up all my things.

Back in my room, I threw everything on the dresser, then turned out the lights and climbed into bed. Only then, staring into the darkness, did I allow my mind to return to Pamela and the evening's conversation. "What do I do, McKale?" I said aloud. "What do you want me to do?"

I fell asleep with those words on my lips.

CHAPTER

Eight

My father used to say, "Pity is
just a poor man's empathy."

Alan Christoffersen's diary

I'm not one to ascribe religious significance to psychological or natural phenomenon. I roll my eyes with incredulity when someone claims a higher power found him a parking spot in front of the local Wal-Mart or a potato resembles Jesus or the Virgin Mother—as if anyone has any idea what either of them look like.

Nor have I ever given much credence to the supernatural nature of dreams. I suppose that my beliefs follow the lines of mainstream psychology—that dreams are just repressed thoughts that slip out at night, like teenagers after their parents are asleep. Having said this, there was something so singularly powerful and peculiar about the dream I had that night that I couldn't help but wonder about its source. I'll leave it to you to determine its origin. As for me, it changed my heart.

I dreamt that I was back out on highway 90, sweaty and hot, my backpack heavy on my shoulders, my legs weary from the day's travel. I was walking the same road where Pamela had fallen the day before. Actually, it was the same time that Pamela had fallen, as I could see her ahead of me on the ground, and myself, crouched over her, helping her. At least that's what I thought I was doing. As I neared I could hear her screaming in agony. That's when I saw that I held a hammer in my hand. I was nailing Pamela to a cross.

I shouted at myself to stop, but neither of the figures in my dream could hear me. I ran to my own side and tried, in vain, to stop my arm. "Leave her alone!" I shouted. "She's suffered enough!"

Just then there was another voice, even more pained than mine. "Stop! Please, stop."

The three of us looked up. McKale was standing in the road ahead of us. She was barefoot and tears were streaming down her cheeks. "Stop," she said softly. "Stop hurting my mother."

I looked back down and Pamela looked into my eyes. "Please," she said. "Grace."

I woke, my sheets soaked with sweat. I looked over at the red digits of the motel clock. It was almost 4 A.M. It took me an hour to fall asleep.

When I woke I took an extra long shower. I sat on the floor of the shower bath and let the warm water flow around me, relaxing my mind. I shaved in the tub, then got out and packed my things. A little after seven I knocked on Pamela's door. It took her a couple of minutes to open.

"Sorry," she said. "I was still getting ready."

Somehow, she looked different to me. Whether the change was real, or only in my mind, there was a difference. When I was a teenager my father told me that when we hate someone we make them more powerful than they are. By that measure, Pamela had been a giant in my life. Not now. Not anymore. The curtain had been pulled aside. She looked small and vulnerable.

"Would you like to get some breakfast?" I asked.

"I'd love to."

The Wall Drug diner served pancakes, fried eggs, sausage, and hash browns for breakfast. I waited for the food, carrying it over to the table when it was done.

"Here you go," I said, setting the tray down. "Breakfast is served."

"That's too much food, but thank you," she said. "How did you sleep?"

I sat down across from her. "I've slept better. How about you?"

"I slept a lot better than I did yesterday."

"I bet," I said. "Considering you slept on the ground without a blanket."

"That was not a good night."

I poured syrup on my pancakes. "Do you still live in Colorado?"

She nodded. "Colorado Springs."

"How far is that from Custer?"

"It's about seven hours."

I cut the pancake with my fork, then took a bite. "So what I want to know is, how did you find me?"

"That took some detective work. I picked up your trail in Cody, Wyoming. The clerk at the Marriott hotel was very helpful."

"How did you even know I was walking? Or where?"

"Oh," she said. "I promised I wouldn't tell."

"You're not going to tell me?"

"I made a promise," she said. "Do you want me to break a promise?"

"Was it my father?"

She just looked at me.

"All right," I said. "Keep your promise." I took another bite. Pamela went back to eating, slowly picking at her food.

After a moment I said, "I've thought a lot about our conversation last night."

She looked up at me.

"The thing is, I've hated you for as long as I can remember. I suppose I just felt it was my moral obligation to hate you—a way of being loyal to McKale. You know, my friend's enemy is my enemy."

"I understand," Pamela said.

"But truth, at least knowing the truth, can change

things in an instant." I looked into Pamela's eyes. "And the truth is, I don't know what I would have done in your situation. But I can't believe that McKale would have been the person she was without those experiences." My eyes moistened. "And I really loved who she was. Some of our most powerful bonding moments were when she was the most vulnerable and upset that you had left her.

"Back in Hill City you asked if McKale would have been mine the way she was if you hadn't been the way you were. The answer is no. And for that I do owe you."

Pamela's eyes welled up with tears.

"You've suffered enough. More than you deserved." I looked into her eyes. "I forgive you."

At first she just stared at me in disbelief, then she began to tremble. Tears rolled down her cheeks. Then she put her face in her hands and cried. I got up and walked to her side of the table and put my arm around her. "It's time to move on. For both of us."

When she could speak, she asked, "Do you think my girl will ever forgive me?"

"I believe she already has."

"You have no idea how much this means to me. I can see why my daughter loved you. You're a good man."

I took her hand. She put her other hand on top of mine. "From the bottom of my heart," she said. "Thank you."

"You're welcome," I replied. "It's my pleasure." It truly was. My heart was full of joy.

After a moment she lifted a napkin from the table and wiped her eyes.

"Now what?" I asked.

"I need to go back to Custer and get my car. I left it in the hotel parking lot. Hopefully they haven't towed it."

"How will you get there?" I asked.

"The woman who runs the motel is driving to Rapid City this afternoon. She says she'll take me. I'm sure I can find a ride from there to Custer."

"Then what?"

"I finish raising my daughter."

I smiled. "That sounds like a good plan."

"And what about you?" Pamela asked. "You'll keep on walking?"

"I'll keep on walking."

She laughed and it was joyful to hear. "You're crazy, you know?"

My smile widened. "That's exactly what your daughter would have said."

We spent the next half hour in pleasant conversation, finding similarities between Hadley and McKale. When we'd finished eating I asked Pamela, "What time do you leave for Rapid City?"

"The woman's leaving after her shift, around five. She said I could stay in the room until then. How about you?"

"I've got twenty miles to cover today. I'm going to do some grocery shopping then start back out."

"Then I won't keep you any longer," she said. "Please stop by before you go."

"I'll do that," I said.

Pamela leaned forward and put her arms around me. Then she turned and walked out of the restaurant. I watched her go, then walked over to the adjacent market—an eclectic store where I loaded up on basics and a few nonessentials, like a bag of cake doughnuts I knew would never survive my journey, and two bags of hore-hound candy, a hard-to-find treat I'd developed a taste for as a kid at Knott's Berry Farm in California. In a moment of weakness, I bought myself a WHERE THE HECK IS WALL DRUG bumper sticker.

I walked back to my room and finished packing, applying the bumper sticker to the back of my pack. I checked the room twice to make sure I hadn't forgotten anything. I felt as if I'd left something there. I guess I had. I knocked on Pamela's door. She opened quickly.

"Ready to hit the road?" she asked.

"Back at it," I said.

"At least you've got the shoes for it."

I smiled. Then I leaned forward and hugged her. "Good-bye, Pamela. Good luck."

"Good luck to you too," she said. She handed me a piece of paper. "That's my phone number and address. If you're ever in Colorado, please come see us."

I put the paper in my pocket. "I'll do that. I'd really like to meet Hadley someday."

"I'm sure she'd like to meet you. Maybe you could stop by on your way back from Key West."

"I'd like that," I said. "I guess we'll see." I ran a hand back through my hair and sighed. "I better go."

Pamela leaned forward and we hugged once more.

"Good-bye," she said. "Be safe."

I slipped my pack on over my shoulders, put on my Akubra hat, then with a furtive smile turned around and began to walk. As I reached the end of the parking lot Pamela called to me.

"Alan."

I turned back.

"God bless you."

I smiled. "Take care, Pamela." I turned, heading back toward the interstate. I sensed that I really was going to miss her following me.

CHAPTER

Nine

As we walk our individual life journeys,
we pick up resentments and hurts, which
attach themselves to our souls like burrs
clinging to a hiker's socks. These stowaways
may seem insignificant at first, but, over
time, if we do not occasionally stop and
shake them free, the accumulation
becomes a burden to our souls.

Alan Christoffersen's diary

Prior to leaving Wall, I had a conversation with the cashier at the Wall Drug gift shop about the road east and she talked me into taking the Badlands Loop, adding an extra ten miles or so to my journey.

My pack was heavy again, as I was assured it would be a while before I would find any decent shopping, so I had filled up at Wall with everything I needed.

Within minutes of leaving Pamela I was back on 90. The morning air was cool and the walking was easy—though I know, in part, because I felt good. In spite of the heaviness of my pack, I felt lighter. Forgiving Pamela had healed a wound I had never acknowledged existed.

Two miles from Wall I exited 90 for Highway 240, the Badlands Loop. It took me half the day, ten miles of walking, to reach the national park.

The road passed through a toll station. There was a seven-dollar entrance fee for "nonmotorized" visitors, and the ranger at the booth reminded me that I could only camp in designated areas. Just a half mile in I stopped to see the first of the remarkable formations.

The native Lakota tribe called the area *Makhóšiča*, which means "bad land." Early French trappers were a little more descriptive, naming it *les mauvaises terres à traverser*—the bad lands to cross.

The Badlands' name is well deserved. The area is a quagmire of slopes and crevices, slick clay and deep sand, all of which encumbered early travelers through the area.

Modern roads carve an easily accessible scenic route through the park, but, by nightfall, I was still a long way from any campground. Despite the ranger's warning I had no choice but to find a place to camp that wasn't designated as such. Near a spot called Panorama Point, I slid down a small ravine where I couldn't be seen from the road.

I ate a can of cold Bush's Baked Beans, an apple, and the last of my Wall Drug cake doughnuts, which were smashed into crumbs.

I started early the next morning. By eight o'clock, I reached Fossil Trail, where I paused to examine some of the prehistoric findings, including tortoise shells and saber-tooth tiger bones. I stopped at Cedar Pass Lodge for lunch and water, but passed by the visitors center because I was afraid I would not make it out of the park before dark.

Near the end of the loop, I came upon a trading post with a giant woodcarving of a woodchuck out front. I picked up a few things for dinner, then sat on the curb next to the giant wood rodent and ate a buffalo hot dog and a bean and cheese burrito that I had warmed in the store's microwave.

Then I headed on toward 90, looking for a place to spend the night. On the service road before the freeway was an abandoned building with its sign still intact:

THE CACTUS FLAT CAFÉ

The windows were all broken out, and the front door was open, leaning on an angle from its rusted hinges. I looked inside. The place was full of trash. I cleared an area to sleep in at the back of the building and spent an uneventful night amid the trash and rodents.

The next morning I backtracked a mile to the trading post for breakfast—a sausage biscuit, cheese Danish, and banana—then returned to the service road.

The day's highlight was encountering a sign that informed me that the movies *Thunderhead*—a 1945 movie starring Roddy McDowall—and *Starship Troopers*—a 1997 movie starring no one—were filmed in the area. Wall Drug billboards were now facing away from me on the opposite side of the highway. They grew sparser the farther I walked from Wall.

All success is imitated, so with the diminishing of the Wall Drug signs, other businesses posted their own, though most of them were homespun and poorly conceived. There's a rule in outdoor advertising: a good billboard should never contain more than seven words, and five or less are preferable. I saw one billboard with seventy-three words. (I was so amazed that I actually stopped to count.) I just shook my head. *Who was going to read that at seventy-five miles an hour?*

I ended the day shy of nineteen miles in the tiny town of Kadoka: population 736. I stayed at the America's Best Value Inn and, at the hotel clerk's recommendation, ate dinner at Club 27. I had the filet mignon with a baked potato. It wasn't nearly as good as the filet mignon I had in Hill City, but I wasn't complaining.

After the last two days of solitude, I was in the mood to talk to someone. Anyone, really. Unfortunately, my waitress wasn't, so I just listened in on other diners' conversations.

The next morning I ate a ham and cheese omelet at the Nibble Nook Café, then started off. The service road had ended at Kadoka, so I resumed my walk along 90 for another five miles or so until another frontage road appeared.

A little after noon an old, loaded-down pickup truck sped by me, close enough that the wind of the vehicle nearly knocked me down. The truck disappeared over a slight incline. About twenty minutes later I caught up to the truck. It was pulled over to the side of the road, its hazard lights flashing, the road around it strewn with an eclectic array of items. I surmised that the truck's cargo had been held in place by a queen-sized mattress, which had flown off.

The driver was grumbling and cursing as he collected his things, which were scattered over a fifty-yard radius up and down the service road, like a big, chaotic yard sale.

The man was a little shorter than me and much wider, probably carrying an extra fifty pounds. He wore a bushy beard and a Chicago Bears jersey. He reminded me of the kind of guy you'd see at a football game, shirtless with a painted face and wearing a rainbow Afro. He glanced over at me after throwing a pillow into the truck.

"Need a hand?" I asked.

He grimaced. "Sure. Why not?"

I slid my pack off and began picking up his things, most of them of little value, including a dozen faded T-shirts, some VHS cassettes of porn, and some plastic dishes—most of them now broken. The man just grunted and cursed.

"Looks like you're moving," I said.

"Got that right," he replied. "Finally got smart and dumped the old nag." He turned and threw a dish rack into the truck's bed. "You know how you spell relief? D-I-V-O-R-C-E. You know what I mean?"

"No," I said.

He bent over. "Then you're not married, are you?"

"No," I replied.

"Then you're smarter than me. Life is short. You gotta grab it. You know what I mean? If you don't look after yourself, who will?"

"You tell me," I said.

"No one. No one looks out for you but you. You gotta watch your own back."

I didn't bother to point out that this was literally impossible. "Where are you headed?" I asked.

"Headed back to where life was good. You know what I mean, back in high school? Chicks and beer, we knew how to live back then. Life was one big party. That's where I'm going."

"Over the rainbow . . ." I said, picking up a couple cassettes with skanky covers.

"What?"

"Nothing. Do you think what you're looking for will still be there?"

He stopped and looked at me as if he was annoyed by my stupidity. "Why wouldn't it be?"

I didn't answer him. We finished gathering the rest of his things, then I helped him lift the mattress onto the heap and we crisscrossed a nylon rope over the mattress and secured it to the truck bed. When the last knot was tied, I picked up my pack. "Well, good luck."

"Thanks for the help," he said. "Can I give you a lift?"

"No thanks. I'm walking."

"Suit yourself." He slammed his door, fired up his truck, which backfired a couple of times, then peeled off, spitting gravel at me. I shook my head. I think of all the people I had met so far on my journey, he was the most pitiable.

A few hours later I came to a building with a sign that read:

Petrified Gardens
"Family Approved Site"
Bring your camera!

I didn't have a family or a camera, but I was curious about this building in the middle of nowhere so I went inside. A bell rang as I entered, and a gaunt, middle-aged man who looked a little like Christopher Walken met me at the door. "Would you like to buy a ticket?"

"Sure," I said.

"How many?"

"It's just me."

"One ticket," he said. "That'll be seven dollars."

I paid him. He handed me a ticket. Then (I'm not making this up) he said, "Just a second." He walked back ten feet to the museum's entrance and held out his hand. "Ticket, please."

I handed him back the ticket.

"Right this way," he said, motioning me forward.

I walked into a long, dark room with displays of mounted rocks behind glass and chicken wire. The room was lit by ultraviolet light, causing the rocks to fluoresce. I stayed there a few minutes, then walked out of the room through a door that led to the backyard.

The yard was scattered with petrified wood, fossils, quartz, and dinosaur bones. There was a "petrified wood pile," also an old cabin, about the size of a utility van, with a sign that read, "Eleven people survived the winter of 1949 in this cabin." At first I envisioned pioneers huddled in buffalo skin blankets, stranded in a blizzard. Then I realized the sign said 1949, the same year Russia got the atom bomb. This place really was remote.

To leave I had to walk back inside the building, where there was a display of fossils, a collection of geodes, and drilled slabs of stone that were somehow used or discarded in the making of Mount Rushmore. The exit led into a gift shop, which had much of the same Mount Rushmore merchandise I'd seen at the monument, and a whole lot of polished rocks set in various accessories: cuff links, tie tacks, key chains, and earrings. I asked the man, who now stood ready as the gift shop attendant, how business was.

"This place has been in the family for fifty-seven years," he said.

He hadn't really answered my question, but I suspected that was probably all he wanted to share. I used the restroom, then said good-bye and headed back to the road.

That afternoon, six miles past the town of Belvidere, I encountered a billboard that read, "1880 Town. *Dances with Wolves* movie props next mile."

I smiled as I read the sign. I thought back to the evening I watched the movie with Nicole. That was also the first night I heard her crying. I wondered how she was doing.

Less than a mile or so later I crossed north under the freeway, to 1880 Town. There was a large, painted wood sign out front that read:

1880 TOWN
DAKOTA TERRITORY
ELEVATION: 2391 FT
POPULATION: 170 GHOSTS
9 CATS
3 DOGS
3905 ~~820 36 6 2~~ RABBITS

The entrance to the town was through a fourteen-sided barn (advertised as the only one in the world). The front fence was flanked by two train cars, an authentic steam engine, and a stainless steel dining car, which, appropriately, had been converted into a diner.

I walked inside the barn where I paid twelve dollars to a grumpy woman with blue hair.

The building was piled to the rafters with Old West antiques and *Dances with Wolves* movie memorabilia—including the sod house and tent from the movie set, the Timmons Freight Wagons, and scores of pictures of Kevin Costner and Mary McDonnell, the woman who played Stands With A Fist, Costner's love interest. I got my phone out of my pack and called Nicole. She answered on the second ring.

"Hello?"

"Nicole, it's Alan."

Her voice was animated. "Alan! Are you okay?"

"I'm fine."

"It's so good to hear your voice. Where in the world are you?"

"South Dakota."

"South Dakota? Have you passed Wall Drug?"

"You know about Wall Drug?"

"Everyone knows about Wall Drug."

"Yes, I stopped there."

"How was it?"

"It was a really big drugstore."

"I've got to go there someday," she said.

"So, the reason I called. Do you remember that scene in *Dances with Wolves*, where Costner hunts the buffalo?"

There was a long pause. "Yeah. I think so."

"I'm standing next to that very buffalo."

"It's still alive?"

"No, it never was. It's an animatronic buffalo."

"A what?"

"A robot buffalo," I said.

She laughed. "Are you sure you're okay?"

"I'm great. Really. How are things? How is Kailamai?"

"She's exactly what you said she'd be. She's a remarkable young lady. She's already enrolled in college."

"How's my dad working out?"

"He's been a lifesaver. We're getting things in order. I'm getting IRAs, mutual funds, and a bunch of things I know nothing about. But who cares about my boring life? Tell me about your adventure."

"Not much to tell you. I'm still on my feet."

"I think about you every day, you know."

I was quiet for a moment. "We had some good times together, didn't we?"

"Yeah, we did. If you ever get tired of walking, there's always a place for you here."

"For the record, I was tired of walking before we even met. But thanks for the invite. I'll keep that in mind."

"I've thought a lot about the time we spent together. I . . ." She paused. "I miss you."

"I miss you too."

"Promise me that I'll see you again."

"I promise."

"Okay," she said. "That will do for now."

"May I talk to Kailamai?"

"She's out with some friends. She'll be disappointed she missed you. She has a whole new batch of jokes she's been saving for you.

"Here's one she told me this morning. A golf club walks

into a local bar and asks for a beer, but the bartender refuses to serve him. 'Why not?' asks the golf club. 'Because you'll be driving later,' replied the bartender."

"That's really awful," I said.

"I know," Nicole laughed. "But it's so funny that she tells them."

"It sounds like the two of you are doing well."

"We are," she said.

"I'm glad to hear that."

"Good. Because you're responsible for it."

"Good to hear I've done something right." I sighed. "Well, I better let you go."

"Okay," she said, sounding disappointed. "Call again soon."

"I will. Take care."

"See ya."

It was good hearing her voice. Still, our conversation reminded me of how lonely I was. I stowed my phone back in my pack then walked out the back door of the barn into the park.

1880 Town was an ambitious re-creation of the Old West, covering more than fifty acres. There was a post office, dentist office, bank, pharmacy, jail, a one-room schoolhouse, a livery full of authentic horse wagons, and at least two dozen other buildings, the whole being even more ambitious than Montana's Nevada City. The most peculiar exhibit was a live, pretzel-loving camel named Otis, who was corralled in a pasture behind the town's church.

I didn't plan to walk any farther that night, so I hung around the town for about an hour, long enough to wander through every building. When I'd seen all I cared to, I walked back to the diner car to get something to eat.

There weren't many other customers, just two families, and I sat at the opposite end of the train car, laying my pack on the red vinyl bench across from me. I looked over the menu, then sat back and waited until the waitress came over a few minutes later. She was young, with short red hair and a badge that read MOLLY.

"Hi," she said. "Sorry for the wait. May I get you something to drink?"

"I'd like some water. A lot of it, like a carafe."

"A what?"

"A pitcher," I said. "A whole pitcher."

"Okay. Do you know what you'd like to eat?"

"How's your meat loaf?"

"It's good. I had it for lunch."

"I'll have the meat loaf and the chef's salad with Thousand Island dressing."

She scribbled down my order. "You got it. I'll be right back with your water and some bread." She walked back to the kitchen.

Outside my window there was a Shell gas station. On the near side of the station was a family sitting on a grass patch next to their minivan. The father was looking at a map spread out over the hood of their car, while the mother assembled sandwiches for the three children. Watching them brought back memories of the family trips we took before my mother died.

My father, like me, was a sucker for tourist traps and probably would have stopped at the same places I had, the Petrified Gardens, Wall Drug, 1880 Town, all of them. As different as I had always thought I was from my father, I was discovering that there was still a lot of him in me.

Molly returned a moment later with a pitcher of water, a tall glass filled with ice, and a small plastic basket with

a mini-loaf of bread and two foil-wrapped squares of butter. "There you go," she said pleasantly. "Your meal will be
right up."

I looked back out the window at the family. The man
was still bent over the map. The woman was now at his
side, her hand resting on his back.

Something about this little drama both fascinated and
conflicted me. The scene was so simple and real, maybe
hopeful, yet it made me feel incomplete. Why did it make
me feel so uncomfortable? As I pondered this I realized
that what I was witnessing had been taken from me not
just once, but twice. First, when my mother died. Second, when McKale did. I was missing my past and future
simultaneously.

Would I ever have what this family had? Would I ever
remarry? Would I ever have children? I honestly couldn't
imagine it. Yet . . .

My thoughts were interrupted by Molly returning with
my dinner. I asked her if she knew of a place nearby where
I could stay.

"There's a KOA about a quarter mile up the road," she
said, pointing out the window. "A lot of my customers stay
there. They have cabins for rent."

"Are the cabins nice?"

"I wouldn't know. But I haven't heard anyone complain."

"Would they complain if they didn't like it?"

She rolled her eyes. "Some people complain if the ice
in their cola is too cold."

I grinned. "You're right."

I finished eating, got a piece of apple pie to go, then
headed out toward the KOA. The campground had several vacancies and the man who ran the place reminded
me that there were no sheets in the rentals.

"There's a mattress but no sheets," he said. "There's a sink and toilet, but if you want to shower you come to this building right here."

"Perfect," I said. Maybe not perfect, but for forty-five dollars a night, with an air conditioner, porch swing, and television, I could do a lot worse. I rolled my sleeping bag out on the bed, turned on the television to the David Letterman show, then lay down and promptly fell asleep.

CHAPTER

Ten

My hair is getting long. I've got to
find a barber before someone
mistakes me for a rock star.

Alan Christoffersen's diary

The next day I did nothing but walk. It seemed like the same scenery kept repeating itself, like the background of a *Flintstones* cartoon. I only passed one house the whole day, until evening when I reached the town of Murdo. I ate at the Prairie Pizza and spent the night at the American Inn.

The next morning I woke with a headache, though it passed fairly quickly. I packed up then ate a breakfast of sausage and biscuits with white gravy at the diner at the World Famous Pioneer Auto Show.

While I was eating, I noticed that the time on the restaurant's clock was an hour different than my watch. I asked my waitress about the time, and she informed me that the time zone changes at their city from Mountain to Central. I had officially passed through my second time zone since leaving Seattle. I adjusted my watch, then walked back out to 90.

I noticed one peculiar thing. I passed a lot of roadkill that day. I don't know why there were more dead animals here than any other stretch I'd walked, but there were. I saw rabbit, deer, badgers, skunk, raccoon, and a few mammals past the point of recognition. McKale used to freak out at the sight of roadkill. She remedied this with outright denial, proclaiming that the deceased animals weren't really that dead, they were just really tired.

Of course I teased her about this. "Look," I would say. "That raccoon is sleeping."

She would nod. "That is one tired raccoon."

"I'd say. He's sleeping so soundly, his head fell off."

I came across the occasional cat or dog, which made me sad every time, knowing that somewhere someone was probably looking for the animal. I thought of the story *The Little Prince*. The only difference between the cats and dogs and the rest of the roadkill was that the wild creatures hadn't been tamed. I suppose that if I were to die out here, I'd be no different. No one would know me. Strangers would think it tragic or horrible; they might scream or call 911, but they wouldn't cry. They had no reason to.

A few people would miss me, but I could count them on one hand: my father; Nicole; Kailamai; and Falene, my assistant who had stuck by me when my business failed. So few. Was this a failed life?

I walked twenty-three miles that day, and counted thirty-six dead animals. I spent the night camped on the side of the road near a pond.

The next day was about the same. I walked twenty uneventful miles, stopping in the town of Kennebec. I ate dinner at Hot Rod's Steakhouse and tried to stay at a place called Gerry's Motel, but I couldn't find anyone to help me. There was a large ice cream bucket on the motel check-in counter with a handwritten note penned in feminine script taped to it:

Tips for Barb
She really deserves it
She gets up early

I waited in the lobby for nearly ten minutes, but neither early-rising Barb, nor anyone else, came out, so I left and stayed at a hotel a block away.

The next day of walking was equally dull. No, more so, illustrated by the fact that the day's highlight was when the shoulders of the road turned from brown dirt to red gravel. At the end of the day, I took exit 260 to Oacoma, a real town with a car dealership and, more important, Al's Oasis.

Al's Oasis was sort of a Wall Drug knockoff, a strip mall with an Old West façade and a grocery store, restaurant, and inn. I ate a roast beef dinner at Al's Restaurant and stayed at the inn for seventy-nine dollars. My room had a view of the Missouri River.

The next morning I crossed over the river, passing the South Dakota Hall of Fame, which I had read about in a tourist brochure in my hotel room. South Dakotan inductees to the hall included TV news personalities Mary Hart and Tom Brokaw, Bob Barker (*The Price Is Right*), Al Neuharth (founder of *USA Today*), and Crazy Horse, though not in that order.

I walked twenty-four miles and spent the night in the town of Kimball, where I ate a basket of popcorn shrimp at the Frosty King and stayed at Dakota Winds Motel for fifty-four dollars.

The next morning, on my way back to the freeway, I passed a sign for a tractor museum. I was tempted, but I resisted the site's magnetic pull and got on the freeway instead.

That evening I slept behind a grove of pine trees planted near the side of the road, which looked like a Christmas tree lot on the edge of a cornfield. I could have pushed myself to the next city, but I just didn't feel like it. I wish I had.

C H A P T E R

Eleven

Heroes and angels usually
arrive in disguise.

Alan Christoffersen's diary

When I woke the next morning everything was spinning. I felt as if I'd just gotten off the teacup ride in Disneyland. I lay in my sleeping bag, holding my head for nearly twenty minutes, hoping that whatever was making me dizzy and nauseous would pass. When my vertigo had eased a little, I packed my sleeping bag and started walking, skipping breakfast out of necessity.

I walked three miles to the town of Plankinton. By then I was feeling almost normal again, so I stopped for breakfast at a convenience store called the Coffee Cup Fuel Stop. A mile later I passed a sign for the Corn Palace.

Ears to You . . .
Visit the Corn Palace. Mitchell, South Dakota

Mitchell was the largest city I'd encountered since Rapid City. I figured that I could reach Mitchell by late afternoon and find a decent hotel to crash in.

During the next few hours, walking grew increasingly difficult, and three miles from the city the dizziness had returned worse than before. Everything began spinning so violently that I was staggering like a drunken man. Then I threw up. I stumbled a few more yards then threw up twice more. I fell onto my knees, holding my head in agony.

I slid my pack off and rolled over to my side. Walking was no longer an option. I didn't know what to do. I hoped that a highway patrolman or a passing motorist might stop to check on me, but no one did. Cars sped past, either not seeing me, or, possibly, not wanting to deal with me. How do you not react to a body lying on the side of the road?

I lay there for several hours, throwing up six more times, until I was dry heaving, the taste of stomach acid sharp and bitter in my mouth. As darkness fell, I was in a quandary. I didn't know whether I should roll farther off the shoulder to avoid getting run over, or stay where I was, hoping some Good Samaritan would stop to help—a prospect that seemed less likely with each passing car.

I had begun to panic, wondering how I would spend the night, when I heard a car pull up behind me. I heard a door open, followed by heavy footsteps. My mind, already spinning, flashed back to when I was attacked and nearly killed outside Spokane. Only this time I was even more vulnerable.

I looked up to see an elderly, gray-haired man dressed in nice but outdated clothing.

"Are you okay?" he asked in a thick accent that sounded to me like Russian.

"I'm very dizzy."

He crouched down next to me. "Have you been drinking?"

I noticed his Star of David pendant. "No. Everything just started spinning."

"Do you have family or friends I could call?"

"No, I'm from Seattle," I said. "Could you take me to a hospital or a clinic?"

"Yes. There is a hospital in Mitchell. I will drive you there."

"I would appreciate that."

"This is your pack?" he asked.

"Yes, sir."

"I will put it in my car."

The man put my pack in his backseat then returned and

helped me to his car, an older-model Chrysler. I moved slowly, holding my head. He opened the door and eased me in.

"Do not hit your head," he said. When I was seated, he shut the door and walked around to the driver's side and climbed in.

"I'll try not to throw up in your car," I said.

He laughed a little. "I would appreciate that."

"No promises," I said.

He started the car. "Are you familiar with the town of Mitchell?"

"No, sir."

"There is the Avera Queen of Peace Hospital on Foster Street. We can be there in fifteen minutes."

I was leaning forward, my hands cupped over my eyes. "Thank you." After a minute I asked, "What's your name?"

"Leszek."

"Lasik?"

He laughed. "Leszek. It is Polish. What is your name?"

"Alan."

"Alan," he said. "It is nice to meet you, Alan."

The ride seemed agonizingly longer than fifteen minutes, as everything in my world was still spinning. Mercifully, the man didn't ask any more questions. He didn't say anything at all until he pulled up to the emergency room entrance. "We are here," he said. "I will help you go inside." He shut off his car and climbed out, then opened my door. He held my arm as I walked with him. When we were inside the building I said, "I forgot my pack."

"It will be safe in my car," he said.

I couldn't believe I was back in a hospital. The smell of the waiting room made me feel more nauseous, and as we approached the registration desk I bent over and threw up on the carpet. Around me, voices seemed disembodied, tinny as a car radio. A woman asked, "What's going on?"

"I do not know," Leszek said. "I found him along the road. He is very dizzy."

"Have him sit down," another female voice said.

A nurse helped me sit back into a wheelchair.

"We need some admittance information," the woman said to Leszek. "I'll need to have you fill out this form."

"I cannot help you. I do not know this man. I just stopped to help. His name is Alan."

"You're Alan?" she asked.

"Yes. My wallet is in my pack."

"We need your insurance information."

"I don't have insurance," I said.

I didn't see her expression, but there was a pause.

"You cannot turn him down," Leszek said.

"I didn't say I don't have money," I said. "I'm not a bum. I just don't have insurance. There's a credit card in my wallet."

"I will get your pack," Leszek said.

I was wheeled back to an examination room. The room's bright lights hurt my eyes.

A nurse with red hair and freckles entered the room about the same time I did. "I just need to check your vitals," she said. She put a small plastic clip on one of my fingers and left it there while she ran an electric thermometer over my forehead and typed in the results on a computer. Then she fastened a blood pressure cuff on my arm and pushed a button. The cuff filled with air, tightening around my bicep. She read the gauge, typed in the results, and took off the cuff.

"What's the verdict?" I asked.

"Your blood pressure is 117 over 78, which is good. Your temperature is normal. I'll need to take some blood."

She walked over to the sink and returned with a needle and a plastic bottle, which she set on the table next to me. "Do you care which arm I poke?"

"No."

"Let me have you put your arm out like this." She ran her finger over my inner elbow until she found a vein. "There will be a small prick . . ." She tapped my arm a few times then slid the needle under my skin. "Okay. The doctor will be in in just a moment. Let me have you slip into this gown. Do you need help?"

"I can dress myself."

She handed me a blue gown that was folded into a square, then left the room. I took off my clothes, pulled on the gown, and lay back on the bed.

I waited about ten minutes for a doctor, a young woman who looked as if she couldn't be much older than twenty.

"Hi, Alan, I'm Dr. Barnes." She glanced down at the paper she held. "Your blood pressure, oxygen, respiration, and pulse are all normal. How long have you been feeling dizzy?"

"It started this morning."

"Were you involved in any physical activity at the time?"

"I was walking."

"Do you do much walking?"

"Yes. I walk about twenty miles a day."

"Very active. Had you been drinking?"

"You mean alcohol?"

"No, I meant liquids. Were you drinking alcohol?"

"No alcohol. I had water. I keep myself hydrated."

"Even so, it's still possible you were dehydrated, walking so far in the sun. Are you on any medications?"

"No."

Her brow furrowed. "Okay. I'm going to run a few more tests. I'd also like to start you on an IV. I'll be back to check on you in a bit."

The redheaded nurse returned a minute later and ran more tests, then disappeared. I just closed my eyes and lay back in the bed, listening to the sounds of the ER flow around me. *Too much time in ERs*, I thought. The doctor returned forty-five minutes later.

"You, Mr. Christoffersen, are a mystery man. You look fine on paper. But then so did my last online date. How are you feeling?"

"I'm still dizzy."

"I think we better watch you for a while. I'm going to put you on meclizine. It's a motion-sickness drug that's pretty effective for treating the symptoms of vertigo— dizziness, nausea. It will also make you very tired. Do you have any problem with sticking around?"

"I don't have insurance, so I don't want to stay any longer than I need to."

"I understand," she said. "Let's get you on the meclizine and see how you react to it, then I'll send you home to rest."

Wish I had a home, I thought.

CHAPTER

Twelve

Leszek has taken me into his home to
care for me. Would I have done the
same for him? I'm ashamed to answer.

Alan Christoffersen's diary

The doctor came back several hours later. The clock on the wall read 1:04 A.M. The meclizine had knocked me out, and even though I had slept most of that time, I was still very tired.

"I think you're okay to go. But you're not safe to drive."

"I can get a taxi to a hotel," I said. "Do you know where my backpack is?"

The nurse said, "Your friend has it next to him in the waiting room."

"My friend?"

"The man who brought you here."

"He's still here?"

"I think he's waiting for you."

I put my clothes back on, and the nurse wheeled me to the lobby. Leszek was sitting in a chair in the corner, not reading or anything, just sitting, his hands clasped together in his lap. The nurse pushed me up to him.

"Ah, you are done," Leszek said, standing.

"I didn't know you were waiting for me."

"Yes, the nurse said you would be out today. I thought you might need a ride."

I looked at him in amazement. And doubt. Maybe my cynicism came from my years in advertising, or maybe it was because of the likes of my cheating ex–business partner, Kyle Craig, but I instinctively tried to figure out what the man's angle could be.

"If you want to bring your car up to the door," the nurse said, "I'll wheel him out."

"I will get my car," Leszek said. He shuffled out of the waiting room.

My eyelids felt heavy. I desperately wanted to sleep and had started to doze when the nurse began pushing the wheelchair out to the curb. Leszek opened the car door, and I stood up and climbed in. He shut the door then got in the other side.

"Where are we going?" I asked.

"I will take you to my house. But first we will stop at the pharmacy for a prescription. The doctor prescribed meclizine, but we can purchase Bonine, it is the same thing, but it will cost you less money."

"How do you know this?"

"The doctor wrote it down here."

We drove to a Walgreens just a few blocks from the hospital. I stayed in the car while Leszek went inside. I dozed off, waking when he returned. He was carrying a small white sack. "Your prescription," he said. "You should be feeling better soon. You just need rest."

He drove me to his house. On the way to his home, he pointed down a lamplit street. "Down there, that is the Corn Palace. It is this town's claim to fame."

"It's a building?"

"Yes, a building. An arena. They play basketball, have concerts and rodeos inside. It is known for the big corn festival. Every year they put up new murals made of corn."

"Maybe I'll walk by it when I leave," I said.

"No, it is not worth the trip." A couple minutes later he said, "We are here."

I had my head down, my hands on my temples, and I slowly looked up. Leszek's house was a humble, redbrick structure with an immaculate yard with pruned hedges and conically shaped pine trees. In contrast, the rest of the neighborhood looked blighted. The home next door looked like a crack house.

He pulled his car into the driveway. "It is not the Corn Palace, but it is home to me." He laughed at this.

"You live alone?"

"Yes. I live alone." He smiled. "No wife to wonder if I have been out with a girlfriend this late at night."

He held my arm as we walked up the concrete stairs to his front porch. There was a green metal mezuzah case affixed to the right side of the door frame. I knew what a mezuzah was because one of my father's clients was Jewish and my father had pointed it out to me once when he took me to his house.

Leszek unlocked his door and we stepped into his front room. The home smelled of some spice I didn't recognize, and the aroma made me feel a little more nauseous. The interior was plain, but tidy and warm, with red shag carpet and a white-brick fireplace mantel. Above it was a picture that looked to be one of those color-by-numbers paintings that haven't been popular for forty years. Most noticeably there was a grand piano that took up most of the room. The expensive instrument looked out of place in the humble home.

"Make yourself at home," Leszek said. "Have a seat on the couch. I will get you some water to take your pills. The nurse said to take another dose before you go to sleep." He left the room.

I slowly sat down. The couch was covered in a dated red-and-gold-pattern fabric, and it sagged a little in the middle. Leszek returned with a glass of water and two pills. "This will help you sleep," he said.

I didn't think I would need help.

I took the pills and popped them into my mouth, followed by a drink of water. The water was warm and I gagged a little.

"Now you should sleep. You can sleep in the bedroom next to mine. My grandson uses it when he visits, so it is a little messy. He is a messy boy. Come with me."

I stood up and followed him down a short hallway. "Here is his room." He turned on a light switch. "He is a messy boy."

The room was actually quite neat. It was small and square, with dark, wood-paneled walls hung with cycling posters. The bed was covered with a patchwork quilt of red and blue.

"It's fine," I said. "It's perfect. I appreciate your kindness."

"We need to make sure you are drinking much water."

"They put me on an IV at the hospital."

"Good. This medicine will make you very sleepy. You will feel better after you sleep. I would offer you something to eat, but I do not think it will be so good for you now."

"No. I don't think I'd keep it down."

"When you wake up, you can eat. If you need something just call for me. I will bring your pack inside the house."

"Thank you."

After he left me alone, I examined the room more closely. There were three posters on the wall, one with a row of cyclists in blue jerseys, with the title Lance Armstrong Tour de France/2005; the second was a picture of cyclists in an array of bright jerseys on a road winding through the Swiss Alps. The third poster was of a beautiful young woman looking through the spokes of a bicycle.

On the dresser was an impressive collection of cycling trophies, one of them nearly three feet high. Next to the bed was a standing mirror in a gold frame and a nightstand with a porcelain lamp with a bright blue shade.

I shut the door, then turned off the light and walked over to the bed. I took off my shoes and lay back on the white, clean sheets. I don't remember much after that.

CHAPTER

Thirteen

Whether cautionary or exemplary,
there has not yet been a life lived
that we cannot learn from. It is up
to us to decide which ours will be.

Alan Christoffersen's diary

I didn't know where I was when I woke. I had had crazy, lucid dreams, no doubt aided by the medication I had taken, but my reality was pretty crazy as well—I was in a city I'd never before heard of whose claim to fame was a Corn Palace, sleeping in the guest room of an elderly, Jewish Polish man I didn't know. That was probably about as unlikely as anything I had dreamt.

I looked around the room. The window shades were dimly lit, as if the sun were barely rising. Considering what time I'd gone to bed, I hadn't slept much. I sat up slowly. There was still some dizziness, but nothing compared to what it had been. At least I could walk if I had to.

I was hungry. I felt like I hadn't eaten for days—which was almost true since I'd thrown up what I'd eaten the day before. I was relieved to see my pack leaning in the corner of the room. I stood up and looked at myself in the mirror. My hair was matted to one side and my jaw was dark with stubble. I opened the door and walked out into the hallway.

Leszek was in the front room reading a book. He set it aside when he saw me. "Oh, Mr. Rip Van Winkle awakes."

"What time is it?" I asked.

"It is almost seven o'clock."

"I only slept five hours?"

He laughed. "No, it is seven o'clock at night. You have slept the whole day."

I rubbed my eyes. "Really?"

"It is true. How are you feeling?"

"Better than I was."

"Is your dizziness gone?"

"Mostly." I rubbed a hand over my eyes. "Seventeen hours. No wonder I'm so hungry."

"I made dinner. I was waiting to eat, hoping you would join me."

"I'd love to."

"Come to the dining room. I must heat the soup. I think soup would be good. And some bread."

I followed him into the dining room, which was separated from the kitchen by a laminate bar. "Please, sit down," he said, walking to the stove. "I just need to heat the soup again."

The table was already set with two bowls, soup spoons, a butter dish, and two teacups. As I sat down a single loud chirp came from a cuckoo clock above the oven, then music started playing as a group of figurines waltzed in tight circles, followed by seven distinct chirps from the cuckoo. The cacophony stopped as abruptly as it began.

"It is seven," Leszek said.

"Your grandson has a lot of trophies."

"He likes to ride his bicycle," Leszek said.

"It looks like he's good at it."

"He rides his bicycle in races around the world. What good is that? He should get a wife, not more trophies for riding a bicycle." He stirred the soup. "You know Rapid City?"

"I walked from there."

"It is a long distance from here, almost three hundred miles. He rode his bike there in one day. He started at four in the morning and arrived in the evening."

I was thinking, *It took me two weeks.* "He is fast."

Leszek brought the soup and bread over to the table. "He is crazy. He rides his bicycle everywhere. You don't get a good wife riding a bicycle."

He ladled me three helpings of soup then pushed the

bread plate toward me. "This bread is good. It is fresh this day from the bakery."

"Thank you."

The bread was cut in thick, airy slices. I took a piece and slathered it with butter, then dipped it into my soup and ate.

"This is delicious," I said.

He got up and went back to the stove, returning with a teakettle. "It is Campbell's Bean with Bacon soup."

"Campbell's?" I ate another bite of bread.

"I have no wife. You expect maybe something fancy homemade?"

"I like Campbell's Bean with Bacon soup. My mother used to make it for me when I was a boy." I ate another spoonful. "I guess you don't really make it. You heat it."

Leszek lifted the teakettle and poured my cup to the brim.

"What is that?" I asked.

He sat back down. "Ginger tea. Ginger tea is good for the dizziness. How do you feel? Are you still dizzy?"

"Not as dizzy," I said.

"I am happy to know this." He slapped his hands on his thighs. "Oh, it is good to have a guest in my home."

"I don't know how to thank you," I said.

He swatted at the air. "I do not need a thank-you. It is good to have the company." He smiled. "You say you walked from Rapid City?"

"I came through Rapid City. But I started in Seattle."

His bushy eyebrows rose in surprise. "You said you were from Seattle. I did not think you had walked from there. That is a long way. Why does a man walk from Seattle to Mitchell, South Dakota?"

I buttered another piece of bread. "To see the Corn Palace, of course."

He looked at me as if he were trying to decide if I was telling the truth. Finally he said, "No."

"You're right. I'm kidding. I'm just passing through South Dakota. I'm walking to Key West, Florida." I took another bite.

He watched me eat, then said, "Key West, Florida. Yes, I know Key West, Florida. So you are like my grandson, you have no wife to keep you home."

I looked up at him. "No, I don't."

He nodded. "So why does a clever man walk from Seattle to Key West?"

"What makes you think I'm clever?"

"You use words that are clever. A man's words say more about a man than his clothes. Because English is not my mother language I am more aware of words that are clever."

"I was in advertising," I said.

"Like to make the television commercials?"

"Yes. But I did more magazine ads and product design."

"Have you made commercials I would know?"

"Probably not. My clients were mostly confined to Washington."

"The capital Washington, D.C.?"

"No. Washington state."

He nodded. "Of course. Of course. Seattle." He took a bite of bread. "Were you good at your advertising?"

"Some people thought so. They gave me awards."

"Is that what makes you good? The awards?"

"No. They are only symptoms of the disease. Not the disease itself."

Leszek laughed. "See, you are clever. But you have not yet answered my question. Why does an advertising man, one with many awards, walk from Seattle to Key West? Plenty of time? Or, maybe, as they say in Poland, you stuck your head above the other poppies, so they chopped you off at the advertising business?"

"No," I said. "I lost my wife."

His smile disappeared. "Oh. I am very sorry. You have divorce?"

I shook my head. "No. She passed away."

He looked distraught. "I am very, very sorry to hear. She was sick?"

"She was in a horse riding accident and broke her back. She died a few months later of infection."

"That is very bad. And now I understand that is why you walk away from your job."

"Mostly. The advertising agency I worked for was mine. While I was taking care of my wife, my partner stole all my clients and forced me into bankruptcy."

"That is bad," Leszek said. "Poor man."

I wasn't sure what he meant by this. "Me?"

"Your partner. He is a poor man. I feel most sorry for him." He stood up. "Let me get you some more soup." He reached across the table and ladled more soup into my bowl. "There you are. Eat plenty."

"Thank you," I said, waiting for him to sit down. After he did I said, "You feel most sorry for him?"

"Yes. He has made for himself a world of no trust. Now he must spend his days afraid for when someone will steal his business. The things we do to others become our world. To the thief, everyone in the world is a thief. To the cheater, everyone is thinking to cheat him."

"That is an interesting way to look at it," I said.

"So what of you?" Leszek said. "Are you free yourself from this man?"

"What do you mean?"

"Have you forgiven your partner?"

"That's not going to happen."

He looked at me sadly. "Then I must feel much sorrow for you too."

"Sorrow because I won't forgive a thief? Actually, he's worse than a thief, he's a betrayer. Dante said the devil reserved the deepest level of hell for men like him." I sat back. "No, I don't think I will be forgiving him."

He looked very distressed. "How can you live your life when you have given it to a betrayer and thief?"

"Some people don't deserve to be forgiven."

"No," Leszek said. "You must forgive everyone."

I gazed at the old man intensely. "You can't be serious. You're telling me that Holocaust survivors should forgive Hitler?"

The man looked at me with a peculiar expression. He clasped his hands in front of him then said softly, "I am."

"You believe even Hitler deserves to be forgiven?"

The man looked at me without flinching. "That is not the question."

"What do you mean?"

"To forgive Hitler, or his *wspólnicy* . . ." He held up a finger. ". . . people who helped him, has nothing to do with Hitler. Hitler is a dead man. Do you believe forgiving him will help him?"

I didn't answer. Of course it wouldn't.

"My friend," Leszek continued, "we chain ourselves to what we do not forgive. So let me say again your question. Should a Holocaust survivor chain himself forever to Hitler and his crimes? Or should he forgive and be free?"

"That's easier said than done," I said.

"Yes, *everything* is easier said than done."

I looked down at the table.

"But you did not answer my question. Should we forgive and be free?"

His question angered me. "Look, I appreciate all you've done for me. You're a better man than I am. But when you know what it's like to have everything taken away from you, then you can preach to me about forgiveness and moving on."

He nodded slowly. "I am sorry to upset you. No, I have not had everything taken away from me." He looked into my eyes with an expression of the deepest gravity. ". . . But only because I was not willing to give up my humanity." He put his arm on the table, then slowly rolled up his left sleeve. At first I didn't see what he meant to show me. His skin was sun-spotted and wrinkled, but then I saw the number tattooed in blue ink on his forearm. I looked up into his eyes.

"I was fourteen years old when German soldiers came for my family and we were put on a train to Sobibor." He looked into my eyes. "You have perhaps heard of Sobibor?"

I shook my head, still a little stunned.

"No," he said, "I think not. For much time no one knew of the Sobibor camps. Even some Holocaust survivors denied it was. But those of us who were there know the truth. A quarter million people died there. Only a few of us survived. I was one of them."

"Where is Sobibor?" I asked.

"Sobibor is in eastern Poland. It was the second camp

built by the SS. It was a death camp. They kept only a few of us alive to help kill.

"The SS was very clever how they ran the camp. They would calm the people by telling them that they were being sent to a work camp. They did this so we would not resist. They did much to make the people believe this trick. They had prisoners in blue outfits waiting at the train station to greet the passengers. When we came out of the trains we were met by smiling bag porters.

"My father believed their trick. He even gave a tip to one of the porters, asking him to have our bags taken to our room.

"Arriving off the train . . ." He rubbed a thick hand over his face. "You don't forget a thing like that. The sound of the train brakes. The smell. There was an awful smell in the air—always that smell.

"The Germans and the Ukrainian guards separated us into two groups—men on one side, women and children on the other, with a space between us. They said that those boys fourteen and under should stay with their mother. I was barely fourteen, I could not decide whether I should go with her or my father. My mother made the decision. I do not know if it was because she had my younger brother and sister and did not want my father to be alone, or if she somehow knew what was to happen, but she told me to go with my father.

"The commandant who met us at the station had a speech. We were all so tired and hungry and thirsty, so we did not think right. We were ready to believe anything. The commandant told us that Sobibor was a work camp. That it would not be easy for us and we were to work hard, but because hard work was good for the soul we should thank them.

"They said that Sobibor was a safe place to be and as long as we did as we were told, we would be well off. But if we disobeyed, we would be punished.

"On the way to the camp a rumor had passed through the train that Sobibor was a death camp, so even as bad as things were, we thought this was very good news."

Tears collected in the corner of Leszek's eyes, but didn't fall, as if he was unwilling to allow them.

"The officer who spoke to the arriving prisoners was an SS officer named Hermann Michel. We called him 'the preacher,' because he was a clever preacher of lies. It is a lesson I learned well, to never trust people with soft voices and guns.

"After he welcomed us to the camp, he told us that there had been an outbreak of typhus at one of the other camps, and since our health was important to him, before we were allowed inside our barracks, we would have to be showered and our clothes to be washed. He told us that was the only reason why men and women had to be separated but we would soon be together and would be able to live together as families. I remember seeing my mother smiling at my father. She believed we would be okay.

"Michel said, 'Fold your clothes and remember where they are, I shall not be with you to help you find them.'

"Then the soldiers walked through the lines asking if anyone knew any trades. They were especially interested in carpenters, shoemakers, and tailors. My father was a shoemaker and I had worked with him since I was eleven. He told the soldiers we had a trade. They took us out of the line. Then young boys walked up and down the line giving people strings to tie their shoes together.

"The old and sick were taken first. They put them on carts. They were told they would be taken to a hospital for care, but they were taken directly to a pit on the other side of camp where they were shot.

"Everyone else was led off in groups past little pretty homes with gardens and flowers in pots. It looked very nice, but it was all part of the trick. They were taken down a path the Nazis called *Himmelstrasse*, the road to heaven.

"After the old people were gone, they took the women and children away. I waved good-bye to my mother and little brother and sister. My mother blew my father and me a kiss."

His eyes welled up again. "I did not know it then, but my mother and brother and sister were dead within an hour. The Nazis were very efficient."

He looked at me and there was a darkness to his gaze. "I heard the screaming once. I had been in Sobibor for three months and I was assigned to weed near the fence in camp two when they started the engines. Even through the concrete walls, the screams escaped. The sound of it froze my blood. It is a sound you never forget. Then they fell off until there was nothing but silence. When I have nightmares, it is that I hear. The silence.

"Sobibor had one purpose. To kill as many people as quickly as the Germans could. When I arrived there, the Germans had three gas chambers, with big truck engines. They could kill six hundred people at a time. But that was not fast enough for them. So three new chambers were made so they could kill twelve hundred people at a time. Imagine—twelve hundred at a time. They were Russian POWs, homosexuals, and gypsies, but mostly Jews."

He went silent and I just looked at him, my heart pounding, my stomach feeling sick. After a moment he rubbed his eyes then met my gaze.

"In Sobibor, there were three camps. Camp one and

camp two were where they prepared food for the officers and guards. Those prisoners who were there cooked or cleaned cars, or washed or made clothing, shoes, gold jewelry, or whatever the guards asked for.

"Camp three was away from us. It was a mystery. One of the cooks wanted to know what was going on in camp three so he hid a note in a dumpling. A note returned to the bottom of a pot. It said, *death*.

"Those who remained alive in camp three had one job, to kill and dispose of the dead. At first the Germans buried the bodies in big holes using tractors, but there were too many, so they began burning them. You could see the flames at night. Always burning. Like hell.

"Once, Himmler himself paid a visit to the camp. To celebrate his great coming, hundreds of young girls were killed in his honor.

"No one was safe. Even those helping the guards would be replaced every few weeks. It was frightful to be told to deliver food to camp three, because many times the deliverers would not come back."

His words trailed off. He had again retreated within himself. My self-pity was swept away by the power of his story. After a few moments I asked, "How did you survive?"

"Hmm," he said, nodding. "People think that the Jews just went like sheep to their graves—and no one resisted. That is not true. Many tried to escape. Many, many lost their lives because of it. The Germans had a rule. If one person escaped, then a dozen in the camp would be shot.

"It was horrible having death hanging over you at all times, but in one way, it was liberating. Once we knew for sure that it was only a matter of time before they would kill us, we had nothing to lose. We knew we all would die, so risk meant nothing.

"While we were planning our escape there came to Sobibor a Russian soldier with the name Pechersky. We called him Sasha. He planned the escape. Some of the men had axes from cutting trees, some made knives, and at the chosen hour one by one we killed the guards and took their guns. It went good until one of the guards was found. Then all was madness. The guards in the towers started shooting down with their machine guns. Our men fired back. It was every man for himself.

"There were forests just past the fence. We knew if we made it to the forest, it would be difficult for them to find us. There were seven hundred of us in the camp and maybe three hundred of us made it out of the camp. But the fields were planted with land mines and many did not make it to the trees. One land mine blew up near me and a man flew past me in the air.

"The Germans radioed for help and soldiers arrived with dogs to hunt us down. In the end, less than a hundred of us made it to freedom. And many of those were turned in or killed by Polish traitors in town."

"Then it was a failure," I said.

"No. It was worth it if even one escaped, because we all would have died—every one of us. I was a lucky one. A good farmer found me. He took me in and hid me until the war was over. I owe my life to him."

I suddenly understood. "That's why you stopped to help me."

"Yes, I made a promise to God that I would never turn away from someone in need."

"What did you do when the war was over?"

"I had much hate. I was asked to testify at the war criminal trials. I got to look some of the guards in the faces and point at them and condemn them. I do not regret this. Mercy should not rob justice.

"But my soul became dark. I trusted no one. I hated everyone. Even the Polish. Until I met Ania." His expression softened as he spoke her name. "My dear Ania. She had suffered too. Not in Sobibor, but she saw death too. Her own father and mother were killed in front of her. But she was not like me. She was so beautiful. Not just her face, which I tell you was beautiful, but in her eyes. Somehow she could still smile and laugh."

When he said this he smiled for the first time since he'd started his story. "Oh, my dear Ania. I could not keep myself from her. But she would not have me. Finally I said, 'Why, Ania? Why will you not have me?'

"She said, 'Because you are like them.' I got very angry. I said, 'I am not like them.' She said, 'Their hate for us—your hate for them, there is no difference. You have such hate in your heart, you might as well have died in Sobibor.'

"She was right. I was just like them. She showed me that the one thing they could not take from me was my choice. So I made a choice to be free of them. To be free of my past, my horrible, horrible past." He nodded. "That's when she married me. That's when I became a free man, even more than when I ran from the camp. In many ways it was the same."

"What happened to Ania?"

"My Ania died nine years ago. After she died I came to America to be with my son. He now lives in California."

I looked down for a long time, then said, "I'm sorry. My problems are small by comparison."

He reached over and put his hand on mine. "No. Your problems are not small. They are horrible too. All the more reason you must let them go." Then he looked me in the eyes and said something that changed me forever. "What would your beloved have you do?"

My eyes welled up with tears. When I could speak I said, "She would tell me to be free."

He nodded. "Yes, just like my Ania. Just like my Ania." He looked me in the eyes. "Honor her wishes and you will honor her."

I pondered what he'd said. "How do I do this? How do I forgive?"

"I had no one to go to. No one to say 'I forgive you.' But you can go to him, your partner. You can tell him you forgive him. But you must first say it to God. Then you may say it to him."

"I don't think he believes he did wrong."

"He knows he did wrong. He knows. But it does not matter. This is your freedom. He must find his own." The moment faded off into silence. Finally he said, "I have burdened you too much for your sickness."

I shook my head. "No. You haven't burdened me. I'll think about what you've said."

He nodded. "Would you like more soup?"

"No, thanks. I'm full."

Suddenly his face lit up. "You would then, perhaps, like to listen to me play the piano."

I smiled. "I would like that."

He smiled wide. "I would be most pleased to play the piano for you."

We both stood and walked into the front room. I sat back into the sofa as Leszek sat down at the instrument. For a moment he looked down at the piano, then he lifted his hands, his fingers hovering briefly above the keys, then he started to play.

I don't know what it was that he played, but I could feel, as well as hear, Lezek's soul pouring out through his music. He was no longer a gray, feeble old man, but vibrant and strong.

Even the room was changed, glorified by the power and brilliance of the music, and I might as well have been seated amid velvet tapestries and gold-leaf veneers in one of Europe's finest concert halls. I closed my eyes and was lost in the passion of the moment—somewhere between anguish and hope, despair and triumph, past and future, nowhere and everywhere.

Then the music stopped as abruptly as it had begun, leaving the room quiet, the silence ringing powerfully.

There were tears rolling down my face. Both of our faces. Leszek was an old man again. He was mortal again. Without looking at me he said, "It is late. I think I will go to bed now." He got up from the bench.

"Thank you," I said.

He turned to look at me. "It is my pleasure, my friend. It is my pleasure."

Then the old man shuffled off to his room.

CHAPTER

Fourteen

To forgive is to unlock the cage of
another's folly to set ourselves free.

Alan Christoffersen's diary

I lay in bed for hours unable to sleep—not just because I had already slept so late, but because my mind was too full. I thought mostly about the horror Leszek had seen in his life. I realized that in some ways the atrocities of the Holocaust had become cinema to me: a mental library of documentaries, movies, and books I had experienced growing up, erroneously believing that I knew something about the horror. I had never met anyone who had lived through it. It was the difference between reading a travelogue and talking to a native.

This was something I could never understand: how could a person be so inhumane to others? I put myself in that equation. Had I been a German soldier, would I have obeyed orders? Statistically speaking, I likely would have. What if I had been in Leszek's position? Would I have attempted an escape or accepted my death? And wasn't that question, in some ways, the very question I was facing right now?

In those dark, quiet hours, I found the truth of Leszek's words. What he said was true—whether I had intended to or not, I had assigned a portion of my future to Kyle. I had deeded him a continual stake in my life—recurring at consistent intervals like a regularly scheduled program in the television network of my mind. As an advertiser, this was something I understood. We paid money to media to lease space in their viewers' minds. That's what I had given Kyle, a television series in my mind, a daily drama I visited, to create pain and hate and justification and . . . Then I saw it. Could it be that I held on to my hate and unforgiveness because I wanted to? That hate was as strong a lust as sex or violence? That I had some carnal desire to beat him mercilessly every day in the boxing ring of my mind? And how long would this show go on before I canceled it? For the rest of my days?

It could. I had met people who held grudges as their most prized possessions, clinging to bitterness and resentment even after the focus of their hatred was dead and buried.

That idea seemed absurd. If my life was, as my father always said, the sum total of my thoughts, then what would such a course of thought make of my life? And was I willing to give that away? No. I wanted to own my thoughts. I wanted to reclaim my mind. I wanted my time back. I wanted to forgive.

I don't know what time I eventually fell asleep, but I woke the next morning around ten. It was light out, so I knew, this time, that it was morning. I didn't feel dizzy. Actually, except for being off schedule, I felt normal. I lay in bed for a few minutes, revisiting the previous night's thoughts.

Long ago I had learned that those middle-of-the-night thoughts didn't always hold up to the light of day. There were times, in my advertising life, when I had jumped out of bed with a campaign idea I thought so brilliant I had to write it down. I kept a notepad next to my bed for that very purpose. I would jump up and scribble down my flash of genius, then go back to bed, only to wake the next morning, read the words, and wonder, *What was I thinking?*

But this time, that wasn't the case. Everything Leszek had said was true. I owned no stock in Kyle's life and I had no desire to vest him with stock in mine. I retrieved my cell phone from my pack, then, as I considered what I was about to do, hesitated. What would I say? How much would I say? In a way, it didn't matter. It was the act itself. The less I said the better. I would call and say, I forgive you. Just those three words. I thought about Pamela. That's what she had come so far to hear. What she had risked her life to hear. But Kyle wasn't, as far as I could tell, seeking what Pamela had. Again, I reminded myself of Leszek's words. It didn't matter. What I was doing had nearly nothing to do with Kyle. How he responded to my forgiveness was up to him. Even if he met my call with hostility, it didn't matter.

Then I remembered that Leszek had said I should first go to God. Surprisingly, calling out to God was harder to me than calling Kyle. What would I say to God? Of course, if God was God, then whatever I said was moot, as he already knew what I would say. I couldn't plan what I was going to say like some kind of presentation, every word carefully scripted, timed for impact. Speaking to God was not about show.

I had once been present at a fund-raising dinner for a Washington State congressional candidate. A minister had gotten up to say a prayer but instead had read a poem. I remember thinking it was a nice presentation, but that it was no more sincere than my last advertising jingle. Maybe it was my father's utter lack of pretense, but I had been taught to say what I meant and get to the point. It made sense to me that I should speak to God in the same way. Keep it simple. I looked up at the ceiling, then said aloud, "God, I forgive Kyle."

Nothing. I felt nothing. I felt worse than nothing, I felt like a liar. I still wanted to beat Kyle to a pulp. I wanted to beat him and leave him on the side of the road like the gang in Spokane had done to me.

That's when I found the truth about prayer. Like Mark Twain wrote, "You can't pray a lie."

I continued my prayer. "God. I want to beat Kyle Craig to a pulp. What he did was despicable. It was vicious and cruel and he is a bad, evil person." Oddly, I felt at peace saying this. Now I was getting somewhere. "I want him to suffer, even as I have suffered." I let the words ring. Powerful feelings began coming to me. "I don't know why he's that way. But I don't want to be like him. I don't want him to be a part of my life. I want to be free of him. I want to be free of this burden. I don't want hate. I don't want *this*."

I stopped and sat in silence. Then I felt a remarkable thing. A warm feeling of peace came over me. "I *want* to forgive him."

That was the answer. Desire. It is not the ability to walk that pleases God, it is the *desire* to walk. The desire to do the right thing. The truest measure of a man is what he desires. The measure of that desire is seen in the actions that follow. "I want to forgive Kyle Craig," I said aloud. This time I meant it.

I picked up the phone and dialed Kyle's phone number. His number had been disconnected. From what Falene had told me back in Spokane, I should not have been surprised.

I put the phone down and thought about what time it was on the West Coast. I had crossed into Central time, so it was only a little after eight. I dialed Falene's number. She didn't answer. I had forgotten that she never answered calls from numbers she didn't recognize. I hung up and tried again, thinking to leave a message. To my surprise, she answered.

"Hello?"

"Falene, it's Alan."

There was a momentary pause. "Alan, where are you?"

"I'm in South Dakota. How are you?"

She paused. "I'm fine," she said unconvincingly.

"How are you really?"

"I've been better," she said softly.

"What's wrong?"

"Do you remember me telling you about my little brother?"

"Didn't he just get out of rehab?"

She sniffed. "Yes. But he's gone back to using. I haven't seen him for eleven days."

"I'm so sorry."

"I'm really worried," she said.

"I'm so sorry," I said again. I didn't know what else to say.

After a moment she sighed. "But that's not why you called. What can I do for you?"

"I'm trying to reach Kyle."

"Kyle Craig?"

I knew this would surprise her. "Yes. I tried to call him but his number's been disconnected."

"That's because there's a long list of people who would like to lynch him. Why do you want to talk to *him*?"

"Part of my healing, I guess. Can you help me find his number?"

"It might take me a while."

"That's okay. You can reach me here."

"Okay," she said. "I'll call you back."

"Thank you, Falene. Now what can I do for you?"

She sighed. "I wish there were something. But thank you anyway." We were both silent for a moment. Then she said, "It's so good hearing your voice."

"Yours too," I said.

"I'll call when I find Kyle's number."

"Thank you," I said.

"I'll talk to you soon."

We hung up. Then I lay back in my bed and looked up at the ceiling.

I missed Falene. After all she'd done for me I wished I could somehow comfort her. She was my truest friend, and without her I doubted that I would still be alive.

CHAPTER

Fifteen

I once heard a preacher say,
"The reason we sometimes connect so
quickly with a complete stranger is
because the friendship is not of this
life, but is the resumption of a friendship
from another." I do not know if this is
true, but sometimes it feels true.

Alan Christoffersen's diary

I lay in bed for a few more minutes, then stood without any difficulty. I was no longer dizzy. *Time to leave*, I thought. I put on some sweatpants and walked out to the kitchen. Leszek was sitting at the table with a cup of coffee, a newspaper spread out in front of him. He looked up as I entered.

"Good morning," he said.

"Good morning."

"I am doing a crossword puzzle," he said. "I am not much good at these puzzles. Do you know a five-letter word for worship?"

I walked over and looked at the paper.

"The second letter is a *d*," he said.

I shook my head. "I don't know. I was never very good at those things either."

"Maybe if it was in Polish," he said, smiling. "But in English, too many words I do not know."

"Adore," I said.

He looked at the word. "Yes. Adore. That is very good." He penciled in the word. "How do you feel today, Alan?"

"Good. I feel good."

"Good is good," he said standing. "I will make you some breakfast."

"No hurry," I said. "Finish your puzzle."

"You will starve first," he said. "I will never finish this puzzle." He walked over to the kitchen. "I never finish the puzzles." He turned on the electric stove beneath a frying pan. "I went to the market this morning. I bought some delicious syrup to go with our pancakes. I like the American pancakes. You say pancakes or hotcakes?"

"Both," I said. "Usually pancakes. But a flapjack by any other name is just as satisfying."

"Ah yes, Shakespeare," Leszek said as he dropped bat-ter onto a skillet. "You are clever." He ran a spatula under the cake, then flipped it over.

"I thought a lot about what you told me last night. Have you written your story down?"

"I am writing it now," he said. "For my children and grandchildren. I do not think my son will read it though."

"Why?"

"I think maybe he does not want to think of such things."

"He will want to read it someday," I said.

"Yes. Perhaps after I am dead. People are always more interesting after they are dead. Especially parents, I think."

I thought of my own father. What questions would I want to ask him once it was no longer possible?

"One of my father's favorite books was written by a survivor of a concentration camp," I said. "Perhaps you've heard of it, *Man's Search for Meaning* by . . ."

"Viktor E. Frankl," Leszek said.

"Yes. Then you've read it?"

He smiled. "Yes, I have read it. I know the writer."

"You've met Viktor E. Frankl?"

He smiled. "Viktor was a friend of mine. We wrote letters."

"That is very cool," I said. "Very cool."

A few moments later Leszek brought the pancakes over to the table. He gave me the top two cakes, leaving a bottom one for himself.

"I have Aunt Jemima syrup," he said.

"Thank you." I poured syrup on my pancakes, spreading it out with my fork. I took a bite. "You make good pancakes."

"Ha!" he said. "As good as my soup?"

I laughed. After we both had eaten a little, I said, "I want to thank you for what you said last night."

"I said too much. Did it help?"

"It did. I tried to call Kyle Craig this morning."

His heavy brow fell. "Who?"

"Kyle. My former business partner. The one who stole from me."

"Oh yes. You called him?"

"I tried. But his phone has been disconnected. But I'll find him."

"Good. Good," he said, nodding approvingly.

"I think it was actually more difficult telling God that I forgave Kyle."

"Perhaps you have not yet forgiven God."

"Perhaps," I said. I knew there was truth in what he said.

"I understand," Leszek said. "When Ania died I was very, very angry at God. I even shouted at him. This to me is most strange, because I did not shout at God when I learned the soldiers had killed my mother and brother and sister, or later when they killed my father. But I shouted at him when my wife died. I think because I could not blame her death on anyone but God." He looked at me sadly. "I think God understands such things."

"You think so?"

Leszek nodded. "I will tell you a story. When my son was very young he found a little knife. I took it away from him so he would not hurt himself. He got very angry and yelled at me. But I was not angry at him." His expression lightened. "I am not saying my Ania was like a knife." He leaned forward and grinned as if he were going to tell me a secret. "Even though sometimes her tongue was very sharp."

I laughed.

"I am just saying that I am older and wiser than my little boy and I understand why he was much upset, so I did not take it so serious. God is older and wiser too. I think he understands too."

This made sense to me. "I hope you're right," I said.

He grinned again. "So do I. Or I am in much trouble!"

I laughed again. As I looked at this grinning old man my heart was full of gratitude. The thought of leaving him filled me with sadness. We ate awhile in silence before I finally spoke. "I'm going to be leaving today."

He nodded. "Yes, I thought you might."

"I would like to shower first if that's okay."

"Yes, of course." He looked sad. "Is there anything you will need before you go?"

"No. You've done more than enough."

"I can drive you back to the freeway."

Even though I had normally refused rides I could not refuse him. "Thank you. I would like that." I took my plate over to the sink and turned on the water to wash it.

"No, no. Just leave it. Please. I will do dishes later. You go shower."

"Are you sure?"

He waved his hands, as if brushing me away. "Yes. Go."

At his dismissal I went to my room, retrieved clothes and a razor, then went into the bathroom. I shaved first then turned on the water and stepped into the tub. There were small slivers of soap in a plastic dish. Leszek was a man who had little and wasted less. I didn't shower very long as I was conscious of using his hot water. I washed my hair twice, still amazed at how long it was. I could almost pull it back in a ponytail.

As I got out of the shower I could hear Leszek playing the piano again. I toweled off, dressed, then went to my room and finished putting my things back into my pack. I made the bed, then carried my pack out to the front room where Leszek was waiting for me. He looked very sad.

"You are ready to leave," he said.

"I'm afraid so," I replied.

"Okay, okay. We go."

We walked out the front door to his car. I threw my pack into the car's backseat, then climbed in as Leszek started the car. As we drove out of his neighborhood, Leszek pointed out the Corn Palace again, its façade adorned with murals made of corncobs. As we crossed under the freeway, I pointed to a small turnoff near the freeway on-ramp.

"How about right over there?" I said.

Leszek pulled his car off the side of the road and shut off the engine.

I felt surprisingly emotional.

"Well, my good friend," Leszek said. "This is good-bye." He reached out his thick hand. I grasped it.

"Saying thank you seems so inadequate. I am so grateful for all you've done for me."

"It was my pleasure," he said. "Is your father still alive?"

"Yes."

"Then he must be proud of such a son. I hope we meet again."

"Me too," I said. "I didn't get your phone number."

"Then I will give it to you."

I took out my journal and a pen. He told me his number and I scribbled it down. "I'll call you when I reach Key West."

"Yes. You call me. I will celebrate for you with toast."

"Toast?" I said. "Is that a Jewish custom?"

"Yes. I will drink toast."

I laughed. Then I shook his hand again and climbed out of the car. "Take care, my friend," I said. "Be safe."

"What so bad thing could happen to me in Mitchell, South Dakota?" he replied.

I laughed again. He waved, then started his car, signaled, and slowly pulled back out onto the road. I watched as his car disappeared in the merging traffic. *All gold does not glitter*, I thought.

CHAPTER

Sixteen

I have discovered the ladies of the
Red Hat Society. Or, more accurately,
they have discovered me.

Alan Christoffersen's diary

Over the next three days I walked from Mitchell to Sioux Falls. My travel was without incident and full of corn. There was corn everywhere. At one point I passed what looked like a petroleum refinery, which vexed me, as it seemed totally out of place amid the acres of cornfields. As I examined the plant it occurred to me that they were making ethanol from corn.

On the first day out of Mitchell, I saw a sign for the Laura Ingalls Wilder home. When McKale was little, she was a huge fan of the Little House books, so I got off the freeway to see the house. Then, shortly past the turnoff, I saw a sign that said her home was more than fifty miles off my course. I turned around and walked back to 90.

I kept on walking. Again, there was a lot of roadkill. On one stretch I counted six "sleeping" raccoons in the course of just one mile.

On the third day from Mitchell, after twenty-four days on Interstate 90, I exited south on 29 toward Sioux Falls. I could see the city in the distance, and even though I was tired, I decided that a good hotel with room service and a hot bath would be worth the extra effort. At nearly twenty-six miles I stopped at a Sheraton.

I decided to take a rest day. For breakfast I ordered eggs Benedict from room service, ate, then put on my swimsuit. I borrowed the terrycloth robe that hung in my closet, then went downstairs to the hot tub.

The hotel lobby was crowded with hundreds of mature ladies wearing red hats and purple dresses, some of them accessorized with feather boas or red or purple fuzzy socks.

I crossed the lobby to the pool area. The hot tub was located on the far side of the pool. Two women were already in the tub, chatting loudly over the sound of bubbling water. They were wearing red hats as well. They stopped talking and looked at me as I folded my robe over the arm of a pool chair and stepped into the water. I closed my eyes and sank into the tub up to my neck.

When I opened my eyes the women were still looking at me.

"Hi," I said.

"How are you?" the one nearest me said.

"I'm fine. And you?"

"Having the time of our lives," said the other woman, who was a little taller and had unnaturally red hair.

"Why are you wearing red hats?" I asked.

"We belong to the Red Hat Society."

"I'm not familiar with that."

"We're just a bunch of dames out for a good time," the first lady said. "You haven't heard of us?"

"Sorry, no. I'm not from Sioux Falls."

"Oh, this isn't just a Sioux Falls thing," the tall lady said indignantly. "The Red Hatters are global. We have more than forty thousand chapters worldwide. We've been featured in *Time* magazine and on television shows. We've even been on *The Simpsons*."

"*The Simpsons?*" I said. "I'm sorry, I guess I've been in a cave for a while. Actually, I've been on a walk."

"That must be some walk," the second woman said.

"I'm walking across America."

"Oh my," the first lady said, "that *is* a walk."

"Really," the second said. "Which side of the country did you start on?"

"I started in Seattle."

"How long ago did you start?"

"It's been nearly eight months. But I got held up five months in Spokane. I got stabbed just outside of the city."

"Stabbed?" the second woman said.

I rose up out of the water to show my scars from the attack.

The first woman put her hand over her mouth. "Oh my. How horrible."

The second woman glanced at my ring finger. "So how did you convince your wife to let you go? Or did she come with you?"

"You lost her," the first said. "How did you lose her?"

I looked at her quizzically. "How did you know that?"

"Yes," the second woman said, turning back. "How did you know that?"

"He's wearing a ladies' wedding ring around his neck," she said. She turned to me. "If you were divorced, you wouldn't be wearing it. If you were still together, she'd be wearing it, and if it belonged to another woman, your wife wouldn't let you wear it."

"Aren't you the Sherlock?" the second woman said. "Is she right?"

I nodded. "She passed away last October. Two days after her funeral, I began my walk."

Both women just looked at me. Then the second woman said, "That's the saddest thing I've ever heard."

"Tell me about the Red Hat club," I said.

". . . Society," the second woman corrected.

The first woman began, "It started when Sue Ellen, our queen mother—"

"You have a queen?" I asked.

"That's what Sue Ellen calls herself," she replied. "The society started when she bought a friend of hers a red hat for her fifty-fifth birthday. There's a poem about a red hat. I won't recite the whole thing, but it goes like this." She straightened herself up a little.

When I am an old woman, I shall wear purple,
with a red hat that doesn't go, and doesn't suit me.
And I shall spend my pension on brandy and summer gloves
and satin candles, and say we've no money for butter.

"And I'll learn to spit," said the second woman.

The first woman nodded. "That's in there too. It means we've spent our lives playing by the rules and being fuddy-duddies, now we're going to kick off our shoes and have a good time."

"And we have *fun*," the second woman said.

"My wife would have been a Red Hat woman," I said.

The first lady shook her head. "She's not old enough."

"She would be a Pink Hat lady," the second said. "Those are our younger members."

"She would do that," I said.

I lowered myself in the water one more time, then rose back up. "I think I'm boiled enough." I stood. "Nice meeting you."

"So nice meeting you," the first said.

"Good luck on your walk," the second said.

"Thanks."

I climbed out of the tub. I dried myself with a hotel towel, then put my robe back on and walked to the elevator. The lobby was not quite as crowded, but still boasted an impressive number of red hats.

As I walked toward the elevator I could see two of the red-hatted women inside. One of them, a very tall brunette with a red fedora, said, "Hold the door, Doris. Here comes some man candy."

I smiled as I stepped in. "Red Hat Society."

Fedora lady smiled. "Red *Hot* Society. And where were you last night at our Red Ball when I was looking for a dance partner."

"I was resting my legs," I said. "I've been doing a lot of walking."

"You look like it," she said. "How about losing the robe and giving us a little peek?"

"Janet!" Doris said.

"Oh, don't be such a prude," Janet replied. "He's probably a male model. He's used to this."

"I'm not a model."

"You could be," Doris said.

"Ought to be," Janet corrected.

"Sorry," I said.

Just then the bell rang for my floor.

"Oh, come on," Janet said. "Just a little peeksy."

I stepped out of the elevator. "Have a good day, ladies."

As the elevator door shut I heard Janet say, "Get his room number, Doris. That man is hot."

The next morning I went downstairs and ate at the hotel's restaurant. There were still red hats all around, but the women seemed subdued, as if a wild night had done them in.

I left the hotel by eight o'clock, getting back on 29 south. The road led through an industrial area and my walk was slowed considerably. I spent a lot of time maneuvering the on- and off-ramps, searching for roads that paralleled the freeway. It was difficult walking, but sometimes there's no easy route.

I had walked for eight miles, to a town with the fantastic name of Tea, before the construction ended and the traffic started to thin out. The landscape turned again to plains, which I was glad to see again. That night I slept under an overpass. It had been a tedious day of walking and I was exhausted. I don't know why some days are harder than others, but I had thought of McKale all day and my chest ached with loneliness. I was glad to finally sleep.

CHAPTER

Seventeen

One cannot judge someone by the
city they're from, any more than
one can judge a book by which
bookstore sold it. Yet, still we do.

Alan Christoffersen's diary

Over the next four days I covered the distance between Sioux Falls and Sioux City with little worth writing about in between. From Sioux City, my next major destination was St. Joseph, approximately 225 miles away. At my current pace I would make it in ten days.

The freeway leaving Sioux City was too busy and too narrow to safely traverse, so I walked along the Floyd River, which was beautiful with its sandy shore.

State lines converged on my route out of the city, and for much of the day I wasn't sure whether I was in Iowa or Nebraska. I could have solved my quandary by consulting my map, but it didn't really matter. I knew I was on the right road, and at the end of the day, that's all that mattered.

Over the next seven days I followed I-29 due south. The road, for the most part, was in Iowa though at times it crossed state lines into Nebraska, as it did in Omaha.

This part of the country seemed old and good to me, reflected, perhaps, in the area's claims to fame. Western Iowa gave us Donna Reed (Jimmy Stewart's low-maintenance wife in *It's a Wonderful Life*), the great orchestra leader Glenn Miller, and the performer Andy Williams of "Moon River" fame—a song I only knew because we performed it on our recorders in Miss Rossi's class in the second grade.

The region didn't just contribute actors and musicians to the American cultural pot. One of the towns I passed was Onawa, the place where Eskimo Pies were invented by a Danish immigrant named Christian Kent Nelson—a schoolteacher *and* candy store owner. (*A delightfully congruent combination*, I thought.) Nelson came up with the idea for the Eskimo Pie in 1920 when a child in his store couldn't decide between an ice cream or a chocolate bar. He ended up patenting the bar and made an agreement with Russell C. Stover, the candy magnate, to produce the frozen treats under the name Eskimo Pie. At the height of their popularity, more than one million Eskimo Pies were sold in America each day. The American dream is made of such stuff.

As I walked, I felt as if I were discovering a side of America that was lost to the media, or at least ignored, written off as inconsequential. As I would discover over the next few weeks, these small towns are tinder boxes for some of the world's greatest people and ideas. Residents from metropolises tend to look down on those from smaller populations—even in their big-city failures. I had an employee from Brooklyn who told me that when his driver's education teacher informed his class that because of all the car robberies their borough had the highest car insurance premiums in the country, some of the students clapped and high-fived each other. Stupid as this mentality is, I don't think it's ever been different. People tend to grab onto whatever they can to make themselves feel superior—whether it's a brand, a football team, or even a locale.

These were not bad days of walking. I passed large, well-organized fields and lilac-strewn countryside, always pleasant to look at, at best, idyllic.

Fifty miles past Omaha, I walked through Sidney, Iowa, the self-proclaimed "Rodeo Town, USA." Sidney is a pert little town with a barbershop, a café, and two law offices—which seemed excessive to me until I remembered a story my father once told me about a town that had only one lawyer, who just about starved until a second lawyer moved into the town and then they both became rich.

In the center of Sidney I stopped at a small grocery store to stock up on food and water. I was the only customer in the store, and the market's lone employee, an attractive, thirty-something woman at the checkout counter, was reading a magazine off the rack when I approached her with my purchases. She set her magazine down and smiled at me. She had short blond hair that framed a pretty, delicate face with striking features, almond-shaped eyes, high cheekbones, and a slightly upturned nose. In contrast to her blond hair, she had brown eyes and dark eyebrows.

"I like your hat," she said as she rang up my items.

"It makes my hair look shorter," I replied.

She smiled. "No. It doesn't."

I smiled back. "Well, at least it keeps the sun off my face while I'm walking."

"Where are you walking to?"

I picked up a package of gum and a tube of lip balm from a display next to the counter and added it to my purchases. "Key West, Florida."

Her eyebrows raised. "Wow. You're a long way from Florida. Actually, from here, you're a long way from anywhere. Where did you start walking?"

"Seattle."

"Seattle." She thought about it. "Then you're about halfway there, aren't you?"

"Pretty close."

"I bet you're halfway," she said. "What's in Key West?"

I shrugged. "Sand, I guess."

"Sand?"

"I guess. That's why I'm walking. To find out what's there."

She smiled. "I like your answer."

"So are there any hotels or bed-and-breakfasts in town?"

"Sorry. Not around here. The nearest one would be in Nebraska City, but you're going the other direction, aren't you? Probably St. Joseph. That's about a hundred miles from here."

"Thank you. I'll just find a place to camp. Is there a park around here?"

She cocked her head a little. "A park? No. But you can stay at our place. My home is nice."

"You've got a yard I can camp in?"

"We do, but I didn't mean you had to camp. We have a guest room."

I was surprised by her offer. That would never have happened in Seattle. "I wouldn't want to impose."

"It's no trouble. Frankly, we'd love the company. It would be the most exciting thing that's happened around here all year. Besides, I'm making spaghetti tonight with Chairman of the Board clam sauce."

"Chairman of the Board?"

"It's one of Emeril's recipes. I'm kind of a fan. Actually I'm a big fan. I love to cook."

"I'd be a fool to pass that up." I looked at her ring finger. She wore a large diamond and emerald ring, set on a yellow gold band. "Are you sure it will be okay with your husband?"

"Matt will be fine. He's really easygoing. He likes people."

"All right. You talked me into it."

She looked happy. "Great. I get off work at six." She looked at her watch. "That's in about forty minutes. If you don't mind hanging around, I'll drive you home with me."

"Thanks. I'll just wait outside."

"You don't have to do that," she said. "Unless you want to. It's not like anyone's beating down the doors." She put out her hand. "I'm Analise."

"Alan," I said.

"It's a pleasure to meet you, Alan."

"Are you from Sidney?"

"No. My husband is. His father owns a couple thousand acres just east of here. He grows corn."

"There's a lot of that going on around here."

"Yes, there is a lot of corn going on around here."

"Where are you from?" I asked.

"I was born about ten miles from here in Tabor. You probably walked through it."

"I did. It was . . . quaint."

"Quaint," she said, smiling. "That's a tactful description."

"Do you have any children?"

"Two. Christian and Casey. Christian's seven and Casey's five."

Just then a woman walked into the store. She was broad and red-faced, dressed in a blue velvet tracksuit. She was huffing as she walked. "Hello, Analise."

"Hi, Terry."

"Just need to pick up some cocoa powder," she said, passing by the counter. She shouted back, "I forgot I was supposed to make brownies for Aiden's den meeting tomorrow afternoon."

"It's in aisle three."

"Got it. Is Christian coming to the den meeting?"

"He'll be there," Analise said. She turned back to me. "Where were we?"

"In Sidney," I said. "Do you know everyone in town?"

She smiled wryly. "I know everyone's *business* in town. You don't have secrets in a town this small." She leaned forward and whispered, "I could tell you things about Terry that would curl your toes."

I looked down the aisle at the woman. "Please don't," I said.

She laughed. "Okay."

A minute later Terry walked up to the counter. She had a box of brownie mix and some canned frosting. She also had a bag of coconut toasted marshmallows.

"So you decided to take the easy way out," Analise said, checking the prices on the items.

"Oh, why go to the bother? I still have to get dinner on. Have any ideas what I could make Ben tonight?"

"Hamburger Helper usually does the trick."

"Yeah, well the doctor told him he needs to cut back on red meat. He's too fat. So what's your secret, doll? You always look like a million bucks in the bank." The woman turned to me. "You tell me, is this woman gorgeous or is she gorgeous."

I nodded. "She is gorgeous."

Analise rolled her eyes. "Please. You're embarrassing me."

The woman was still looking at me. She stuck out her hand. "Terry Mason, just like the old TV show."

"You mean, Perry Mason?"

"Exactly. How do you do?"

I took her hand, wondering what could be so scandalous about this woman as to curl my toes. "Alan Christoffersen."

"You visiting or just passing through?"

"Just passing through," I said.

"Maybe you should stay awhile. The rest of America may be going to heck in a handbasket, but Sidney is a rock in the storm. A jewel in America's crown."

"Mr. Christoffersen is walking across the country," Analise said.

"Oh, Lord. Maybe I should send Ben with you. He'd have to walk from sea to shining sea to get back to his fighting weight." She turned back to Analise. "What are you cooking tonight, darling?"

"Spaghetti with clam sauce."

"Well ain't you fancy, cooking all ee-tal-yun."

"It's one of Emeril's recipes."

"Well you know I love Emeril on occasion, but give me Paula Deen any day. That woman ain't afraid of butter."

Analise laughed. "No, she's not. That will be six forty-nine."

"Here you go," she said, handing her a bill.

"Out of ten. That's three and fifty-one back."

"Keep the penny in that little dish, honey."

"Okay."

"Casey's diarrhea under control?" Terry asked.

Analise blushed. "Yes. Has been for some days."

"Did you try carrot soup? Carrot soup and brown rice works wonders with the squirts. But so does turmeric."

"She's fine. I just got some Imodium."

"That works too. Tell Christian not to forget to bring his kerchief to the pack meeting, we're making kerchief rings. Have a good night." She turned back to me. "You too, Mr. Christensen. I wish you well on your walk."

"Thank you," I said, smiling a little.

She walked out. Analise sighed. "Like I was saying, Mr. Christensen. There are no secrets in Sidney."

"Clearly."

At five minutes after six another woman walked into the store. She was younger than Analise, and wore tight Wrangler jeans and an open shirt with a tube top underneath. "Sorry I'm late, Lise. Rush-hour traffic."

"Rush hour in Sidney's a bear," Analise said. "Don't worry about it. Ciao."

"Have a good night," the young woman said to Analise, glancing at me suspiciously.

"Let's go," Analise said. She picked up her purse and a plastic bag with groceries.

"May I help you with that?" I asked.

"Thanks."

She handed me a plastic bag, which contained spaghetti, a loaf of French bread, and cans of tomato sauce, then I followed her out to a brown Ford Ranger truck. "This would be my transportation," she said, opening the door by remote.

I threw my pack in the truck's bed and climbed in the passenger side.

Analise turned the key in the ignition and the *Moulin Rouge* soundtrack came on. She reached over and turned off the CD player.

"I live just a mile from here." She backed out of the stall then pulled a U-turn in the middle of Main Street.

I thought back to the young woman's excuse for being late. "Rush-hour traffic?" I said.

She nodded. "It's code for her boyfriend. His name is Rush."

Analise's home was surprisingly large and beautiful, a two-story Folk Victorian house painted pale yellow with white trim, dark red shutters, and a ground-level wraparound porch. A large American flag hung from one of the porch's posts.

"Your home is beautiful," I said. "My wife would have loved it."

"You're married?"

"I was. She passed away."

Analise looked at me with real sympathy. "I'm so very sorry."

She pulled the truck up to the side of the home, and we both got out. I pulled my pack from the truck's bed while Analise waited for me. As we approached the front porch, a little girl came running out. "Mama!"

"Hi, Case." Analise squatted down and hugged the girl. "How was school?"

"Boring," she said. "And Kyle picked his nose in front of everyone."

"Well that doesn't sound boring," she said, standing back up. She looked at me and smiled. "The glamorous life of a mom."

"Who are you?" Casey said to me.

"I'm Alan."

"Alan?"

"Mr. Christoffersen," Analise said.

"Hi, Mr. Christoffersen. Are you going to have dinner with us?"

"I think I am," I said.

She smiled. "Good." She turned and ran into the house.

Analise and I followed after her. I could hear the girl shouting, "Christian, Mommy's home. And she brought someone."

Analise turned to me, brushing a strand of hair from her face. "Sorry, it's big news when someone visits. We don't get many visitors this far from Earth."

We stepped inside the house.

"I'm sorry, it's messy. I've been working extra lately."

"This is really beautiful," I said.

She smiled. "Thank you. The guest room is right here next to the den. You're probably tired. If you'd like to rest or wash up, it will take me about forty minutes or so to get dinner on."

"When does your husband get home?"

"You never know," she said. "The work of a farmer never stops. Working for family makes it worse. I've stopped waiting for him."

"I'd be happy to help you cook. I'm not a bad cook. I mean, I'm not Emeril, but I can boil water."

She nodded. "Great. You're hired. The kitchen is right through that door."

"I'll go wash up," I said.

I carried my pack into the room Analise had pointed to. The guest room was quaint and tidy, the kind of room you'd expect in a bed-and-breakfast. It had a high-mattressed canopy bed with white carved posts. There were pictures of the children on the wall. The largest picture was a portrait of the entire family. I figured the photograph was fairly dated as Casey was still a toddler. Matt, Analise's husband, was tall and muscularly built. I thought he looked more cowboy than farmer. He was handsome. In fact, the whole family was rather attractive.

I washed my hands and face, then found my way to the kitchen. Analise had put on an apron and was standing at the stove frying something in a skillet. Next to her was a large pot with a high flame beneath it. The room already smelled wonderfully of garlic.

"Smells delicious," I said. "What would you like me to do?"

"Would you mind helping me fry the garlic?"

"No problem," I said.

She stepped away from the stove. "Great. I'll get the clams and pepper ready. The garlic's only supposed to cook for a few minutes. When you're done, we add crushed red pepper and clams then cook for two more minutes." She walked over to the counter and put the clams and peppers in a bowl, then brought them over to me. "The garlic should be about ready."

"It looks ready," I said.

She poured her bowl into my pan. The clams sizzled loudly. "Okay, do you know how to sauté?"

"Just stir, right?"

"Right." She left, then returned with a cup of white wine, which she also poured into my pan. "All right. Just let that cook until the wine reduces a little, then we add the tomato sauce. I'll get the pasta going." She opened a package of spaghetti and dropped it into the boiling water.

"I think it's ready for the tomato sauce," I said.

She glanced over. "I think you're right. Just pour it all in."

I took the can and added the sauce to the sizzling mixture. The aroma was delicious.

"How long do I let it cook?" I asked.

"According to Emeril, just until the clams start to open." She looked at me. "You're from Seattle; you probably cook clams all the time."

"No," I said. "But I do love a good chowder."

She stirred the noodles a little, then went to the door and shouted, "Casey, come here."

A moment later the little girl walked into the kitchen. "What, Mama?"

"Where's Christian?"

"He's in his room. He's playing video games."

"Will you tell him to come down and help you set the table?"

"Okay."

A few minutes later she returned with her brother in tow. Christian had long, blond hair and an excessive frown. "I was playing Xbox."

"It's time to eat."

"I'm not hungry."

"I didn't ask," she said. "Help Casey set the table."

He rolled his eyes and walked out. Analise shook her head. "You can't live with them, you can't lock them up in cages in the basement."

She put on oven mitts, then squatted down at the oven and brought out a pan of garlic bread. She set the pan on the counter and stacked the bread on a plate. Then she lifted a piece and held it up to my mouth. "Try this."

I went to take a bite but she pulled it away from me. "It's hot," she said. "You've got to blow on it first."

I blew on the bread, then took a bite. "That's good."

"I use garlic salt, then add Parmesan cheese." She took a bite as well then set the piece on the counter. "The pasta should be done." She stuck a wooden fork into the pot and lifted out a noodle, dangling it into her mouth. "Perfect. Al dente."

"Al dente?"

"*To the teeth*. It means it's not overcooked. Now, if you'll take the bread out to the table, I'll drain the pasta."

I took the plate of bread out to the dining room. Casey was putting the silverware next to the plates while her brother sat on the ground by the wall playing a handheld video game.

"Christian won't help," Casey said.

"Of course he will," I said. "Won't you."

He didn't look up from his game. "No."

I set the bread on the table. "C'mon, Christian," I said. "Give your sister a hand."

He looked up, glaring at me. "Who are you?"

"I'm Alan."

"You're not my boss, Alan." He returned to his game.

Honestly, my first instinct was to smack the kid, but I doubted that would fly with his parents. So, being unsure of how to handle the situation, I just went back to the kitchen. Analise was in the middle of draining the pasta into a plastic colander in the sink. Steam was rising up around her.

"Need a hand?" I asked.

"No, I got it." She poured all of the pasta out, leaving some water in the pot. "You always save a little of the water, in case the noodles get too dry."

"Got it," I said. "Emeril?"

She nodded. "Emeril." She carried the colander over to the stove, where she mixed the pasta in with her clam sauce. Then she turned to me with a satisfied smile. "It's ready."

She poured the pasta into a large ceramic bowl and we both went out to the table.

Christian smirked when he saw the pasta.

"Can I have Cap'n Crunch tonight?"

"No."

"Can I have Lucky Charms?"

"No. You can't have any cereal. I made spaghetti."

"It looks gross. It looks like puke."

Analise blushed. "Don't talk like that."

"You can't make me eat it."

I could tell Analise was doing her best not to lose her temper.

"You're going to eat it."

"No I'm not."

"Then you can go to your room hungry. Go."

He glared at her then pushed away from the table. "Fine. I didn't want to eat that crap anyway." He glanced over at me hatefully then stormed up the stairs.

"He's mean," Casey said.

Analise was embarrassed. "I'm sorry," she said to me.

"I couldn't handle it," I said.

"What?"

"Being a parent."

"Well, apparently neither can I," Analise said.

"You're a good mommy," Casey said.

Analise smiled wryly. "Thanks, sweetie. Would you mind saying grace?"

"Okay." She reached over and took her mother's hand. Analise reached over and took mine. "God is good, God is great. Bless the food we eat. Amen."

"Amen," I said.

"Amen," Analise said. "Thank you."

"Anytime, Mama."

I grinned. Casey really was a cute girl.

Analise dished the pasta out onto our plates. It was delicious, though probably a bit exotic for a kid's palate. After a few minutes Casey said, "Mom, can I be done?"

Analise looked at Casey's plate. "You didn't eat very much."

"Sorry."

"Don't you like it?"

She didn't say anything. Analise sighed. "All right. Why don't you make yourself a peanut butter sandwich? Take one to Christian too."

"Okay."

"Then get ready for bed. Don't forget to brush."

" 'Kay."

When Casey was gone Analise turned to me with a look of exasperation. "Why do I bother?"

"Kids don't know what's good," I said. "When I was little, my neighbor had an avocado tree. We thought they were the grossest things on the planet. We used to just throw them at each other. Now I pay two dollars for one."

"I know. They'd be happier if I just poured them a bowl of cereal every night. It would make my life a lot easier."

"Your husband might have something to say about that."

She frowned. "The thing is, it's not like I'm taking the easy way out. I get home from work and I'm exhausted, but then I cook and do the dishes. It's never-ending."

"It's like they say, 'A mother's work is never done.' "

"Only when you die," Analise replied. "Then you have eternity to think about everything you did wrong and how you screwed up your children."

"You sound like an argument for birth control."

"There are times I think Planned Parenthood could follow me around with a camera and use the video to keep young women from getting pregnant."

I grinned. "Well, I think you do a really good job. Does your husband help out much at home?"

She looked like she didn't like the question. "When he's around," she said.

"For the record, your spaghetti is fantastic. Emeril couldn't have made it better himself."

She smiled at this. "You think?"

"Bam!" I said.

She laughed. "You really do know who Emeril is. I thought you were pretending."

"I haven't always lived in a cave," I said. "I even know who Paula Deen is."

"Now I'm really impressed." She looked down at my empty plate. "Would you like more pasta?"

"I would, but I usually try to stop after my third helping."

"Okay." She looked at me. "Do you mind if I ask you something about your wife?"

"No."

"If you don't want to talk about her, I understand."

"It's okay."

"How did you lose her?"

"We lived in a suburb with a horse trail. She was riding one day and the horse got spooked and threw her. She broke her back."

Her expression showed her distress. "I'm so sorry. Was she killed instantly?"

"No. She got an infection. She died a month later."

"I'm so sorry," she said again. She looked down for a moment. "I've wondered if it's better to watch a loved one die over time, or to just lose them—never saying what you would have liked to say."

"Watching her die wasn't easy. But we said everything we needed to say. I guess if I had to do it again, I would choose to have that extra time together. But she was the one in pain, so I guess I'm selfish."

"I don't think that's selfish. I think it's beautiful." She looked down at her plate. "I think I would choose the time too."

The conversation stopped, swallowed into a cloud of

sadness. After a moment Analise said, "That kind of killed the mood. I'm sorry I brought it up."

"No, it's good to talk about it sometimes. I carry a lot of emotions and I never have a chance to let them out. Sometimes I think I'm going to explode."

"How long was it after she passed away that you decided to walk?"

"Two days after her funeral. While I was taking care of her, I lost my business and our home was foreclosed on. The day after her funeral the bank gave me notice that they were taking my home."

"That's horrible."

"Yeah, it was. I had nothing holding me there anymore so I just packed up and started to walk."

"I know I asked you before, but really, why Key West?"

"It was the farthest place on the map."

She let my words settle. Then she said softly, "I understand better than you know." She forced a smile. "So before you started your walk, what did you do?"

"I owned an advertising agency."

"That's the business you lost?"

I nodded. "Yes."

She suddenly smiled. "Did you wear your hair that long when you were a businessman?"

"No, believe it or not, I used to look respectable. Short hair, clean-shaven, Armani suits, and Brooks Brothers button-downs, heavy on the starch. You kind of let things go when you're on the road."

"It works, though. I think it's rather rugged-looking. You look like one of those guys on the covers of the paperback romances we sell at the store."

"You're saying I look like Fabio?"

She cocked her head with a wide grin. "Maybe a little. You're not Italian. And you're not as buff."

"I'm not as buff as Fabio?"

"Don't get me wrong, you're in good shape, but just not . . ."

"I know. Fabio buff."

She smiled wryly. "Sorry."

"So I'm not Fabio," I said. "But I can do two things he can't."

She leaned forward. "Do tell."

"First, I can use words with more than one syllable. And second," I said, pausing for dramatic impact, "I do dishes."

She gasped. "Wow. That is hot. I think you just edged out Fabio."

"I thought so," I said.

"Really? You do dishes?"

"Yes, I do. Come on," I said, standing. "Let's get them done."

She stood. "You really don't have to help."

"Oh, good, because for a second there I thought you had a gun to my head and were *making* me do the dishes. Since you don't, I'll just go read or something while the exhausted, full-time working mother of two children who made the incredible dinner and invited me to stay in her home cleans up after me. Yes, I'll feel really good about that."

Analise laughed. "All right, you made your point. You wash, I'll dry and put away."

We carried our dishes to the kitchen, then, as she filled the sink with hot water, I cleared the rest of the table.

"What do you want to do with this?" I said, carrying in the half-full bowl of pasta.

"We'll just put Saran over it and put it in the fridge. The wrap's in that drawer right there, third down."

I squatted down to the drawer. "Did you want to make a plate for your husband first?"

She looked at me quizzically. "What?"

"I thought maybe you would want to . . ." As I looked at her, I suddenly understood. I stood up, setting the bowl aside. "There is no husband . . ."

She didn't answer at first. Then she said, "Of course I have a husband. There's a picture of us in your room."

"It's an old picture."

She didn't say anything.

"What happened to him?"

She just stood there, looking at me anxiously. Neither of us spoke for what felt like minutes. Then she shook her head. "I'm sorry. I . . ." She took a deep breath, then slowly exhaled. "I couldn't really invite some strange man into my home."

"The picture in my room . . ."

"That was taken three weeks before he was killed. Three years ago."

"How was he killed?"

"Working. He was in a combine accident. He went to work one day and never came back."

Suddenly everything made sense. Her interest in McKale. Our discussion about losing a loved one suddenly or over time. Her son's behavior.

"How is your son dealing with it?"

"He's very angry. I think he blames me sometimes. I know it's not rational, but he's a kid."

"How are you taking it?"

She shook her head. "Not well. You know what it's like.

I can see why you would want to walk away. It's been hard living here in this little town."

"Why don't you move?"

"I have no place to go. My friends are all here or in Tabor, and my siblings are all in the same financial boat that I'm in. My parents can't help. They lost their farm a few years ago and are now living on welfare in Omaha. I would be too if it wasn't for Matt's parents. We didn't have any life insurance. Matt said it was just a waste of money, since his parents have so much money and if anything happened, they'd take care of us."

"And they do?"

"Yes. But it comes at a price. They won't let me leave."

"How can they stop you?"

"How can they not? If I leave, they'll cut me off."

"They told you that?"

"Directly," she said.

"Could you sell your house?"

She shook her head. "Not in this market. Believe me, there's not a lot of people moving into Sidney. Besides, my in-laws own the house. We borrowed the money from them." She sighed. "I'm stuck. I have no skills, so I'd be working full-time just to survive in some dingy apartment while someone else raised my kids."

"I don't mean to be crass, but you could remarry."

"Not in Sidney. The men are either married, twice my age, or there's a clear reason why they're not married. I'd just be trading one problem for another."

"So you're stuck."

She nodded. "My in-laws want me to be stuck. A friend told me that my mother-in-law told her mother that they didn't want me to remarry. They thought it would be too confusing for the kids and she was afraid I might take their grandchildren away. But I think there might be even more to it than that. My in-laws were really broken by Matt's death. My father-in-law, Hank, was driving the combine when Matt was killed. I think he blames himself.

"What makes it even more complex is Hank's own father died young and his mother never remarried. From things he's said, I think he believes that remarrying would be dishonoring Matt. So, they financially force me into doing what they want."

"That's not right," I said.

"No, it's passive-aggressive. It's how Hank and Nancy get their way and still sing in the choir every Sunday with a clear conscience." She sighed. "I'm sorry to unload this on you. It's just so good to have someone I can talk to. There's no one here I could say that to without it getting back to them. I'm sorry that I lied to you."

"No, you're in a tough spot. I understand."

We both stood there a moment in silence. Finally, Analise looked around the kitchen and untied her apron. "It's late. I'll finish the dishes in the morning. I take the kids to school early then go to work, so if you decide to sleep in, just help yourself to breakfast. There's fruit and yogurt in the fridge and cereal in the cupboard."

"All right," I said. "Thank you."

She gazed at me for a moment, then smiled sadly. "Good night, Alan. It was nice visiting with you."

"Good night, Analise. Thank you for everything."

She laid her apron on the table, then with a last, furtive glance at me, went upstairs to her bedroom. I walked to my room and went to bed.

CHAPTER

Eighteen

The trapped are less concerned
with rules than escape.

Alan Christoffersen's diary

I don't know what time it was when I woke. I'm not usually a light sleeper, but I woke to a dim light coming from outside my room. I looked over. Analise stood in the doorway, her petite figure silhouetted by the light from the foyer. She quietly shut the door, then walked over to the side of the bed. I lay there looking up at her. She was breathing heavily, but said nothing.

"Are you okay?" I asked.

For a moment she just looked at me. Then she knelt by the side of the bed. My room was bathed in the moon's blue glow and I could see her eyes, dark and lonely and filled with hurt. "No. I'm not." She took a deep breath. Then staring intently into my eyes, said, "Will you make love to me?"

For a moment I just stared at her. She looked vulnerable—beautiful, lonely, and vulnerable. My body screamed for her, but I slowly shook my head. "No."

She lowered her head. After a moment she asked, "Aren't I pretty enough?"

"It's not that," I said.

"Then what is it?"

"You're not mine."

She touched my arm. A tear rolled down her cheek. "I'll be yours tonight," she whispered. "I won't ask anything of you. I won't hold you to anything. I promise."

I propped myself up on my elbow. "Analise . . ."

"I just want someone to love me."

I looked into her eyes. "I understand. But I can't."

After a moment she wiped her eyes with the back of her hand. "I'm sorry. I'm so embarrassed."

"Do you want me to go?" I asked.

She was looking down, but shook her head. "No." She rubbed her eyes. "You must think I'm horrible."

"No. I don't."

She knelt there for another moment, then sighed and stood. "Good night." She started to the door.

"Analise," I said.

She stopped, slowly turning back. Her face was wet with tears.

"Come back."

She just looked at me.

"Come here. Please."

She walked slowly over to the side of my bed. I moved over, making a space for her. "Let me hold you."

"But . . ."

I pulled down the sheets then took her hand. "Lay down. I just want to hold you." She sat on the side of my bed then lifted her legs onto the bed next to me. I put my arms around her, pulling her tightly in, our faces next to each other. I whispered into her ear, "I know what it's like to feel so lonely that you just don't care anymore. You're a good girl, you just hurt. I understand. I hurt too. I want you too. But I'm not ready to share what belonged only to McKale and me."

She was staring into my eyes. Then it was as if some great emotional dam burst, because she began sobbing so hard that the bed shook. I held her tightly until her sobbing slowed to a whimper. Finally she stilled and fell asleep.

I leaned over and kissed her cheek. "You are so beautiful," I said. I lay back and fell asleep too.

CHAPTER

Nineteen

She is a rose, blooming amidst cornfields.

Alan Christoffersen's diary

I woke the next morning to the first rays of dawn stealing through the room's window. Analise was facing me, her eyes open. She looked soft and peaceful.

"Thank you," she said, in a voice only slightly above a whisper, her breath warm on my face.

"For what?" I asked.

"For saying no and for holding me."

"You're beautiful," I said.

"So are you." She paused. "Do you think I'll ever see you again?"

"I don't know."

"I hope so. I hope someday you come back on a white horse and save me."

"Analise . . ."

She put her fingers on my lips to still them. "A girl needs her fantasies." She laid her head against my chest, and I pulled her tight against me. Her warmth and softness were exquisite. She wasn't McKale, but she was lovely.

After a few minutes Analise groaned slightly as she pulled away. "I better get up before the kids wake."

"Wait," I said. "What are you going to do now?"

"Get the kids ready for the day."

I laughed. "I was thinking a little broader."

"Like with my life?"

I nodded.

"I don't know. But I feel so much better. I haven't felt this peaceful since the day before Matt died."

"You loved him," I said.

"With all my heart." She touched my face. "I'm glad your walk brought you through Sidney, Mr. Christoffersen."

"So am I."

She leaned forward and kissed my cheek, then climbed out of bed. She looked back from the door. "Bye."

"Bye."

She walked out, pulling the door shut behind her. I sighed, then lay back and looked at the ceiling. Then I got up and showered.

When I walked out of the room the two children were eating bowls of cereal, staring at the backs of the cereal boxes in front of them. Casey turned around and looked at me. "Hello, Mr. Christoffersen."

"Hi, sweetie."

"Are you going to be here tonight?"

"No. I'm going back out walking."

She frowned.

Christian wouldn't look at me.

"Hey, Christian," I said.

"What?"

"I have something for you."

He turned and looked at me. "What?"

I took my Swiss Army knife out of my pocket. "I thought you could use this."

He sat there staring. I could tell he wanted it, but wasn't sure how to accept the gift. I walked to the table and set it down next to his bowl. "It will come in handy with your Scouting."

He nodded.

"Better not take it to school, though. I'm sure they frown on students bringing knives to school."

He nodded again.

"Okay, you take care."

He still didn't say anything.

A few minutes later Analise walked into the dining room. She grabbed the milk carton. "Okay, kids. Run out to the car. I'll be right out. Christian, don't forget your pack."

"Okay," he said. Then he looked at me. "Thanks, Alan." He grabbed the knife then walked over and picked up his pack.

Casey ran over and hugged me. "Good-bye, Mr. Christoffersen. Thanks for visiting."

I smiled. "It was my pleasure."

She went back and got her pack, then both kids walked out the front door.

Analise looked at me curiously. "What was that about?"

"Casey's a sweet little girl."

"No, with Christian."

"I gave him a present. I hope it's okay. It's a Swiss Army knife."

She shook her head. "He's been asking for one for almost a year. I keep telling him no."

"Sorry," I said.

She grinned. "It's okay. I'm just overprotective. Thank you for doing that for him."

"You're welcome."

"Just a minute." She left with the carton of milk, then returned. She walked up to me. "I don't know what to say. I can't believe I feel like I'm going to cry. I don't even really know you."

"You know me better than you think. We belong to the same club."

She nodded. "I wish I could revoke my membership."

"We all do."

She stared into my eyes. "Thank you for giving me hope." She took something out of her pocket. "Will you take this to Key West with you?"

"What is it?"

"It's the bracelet I was making when I learned of Matt's death." It was a simple black cord with a small pewter oval that said, *Believe*.

I closed my hand around it. "Thank you."

"You're welcome. If you think of it, look me up sometime. You know where to find me." We embraced. Then she looked into my face, wiping the tears from her eyes. "Bye."

"Bye, Analise."

She walked to the door, then turned around. "Just lock the door behind you."

I nodded and she walked out. I went out to the porch and watched her climb into the truck. She glanced at me as she backed out. Casey waved. So did Christian. Then she drove away.

I took a deep breath, exhaling slowly. I wondered if I would ever see her again. I examined the bracelet she'd given me and put it on my wrist. Then I went back inside. I grabbed a banana from the counter, then lifted my pack up over my shoulders, and stepped back out onto the porch. I checked the door to make sure it was locked and pulled it shut.

At the edge of the yard I stopped and looked back at the house. *Just another story under the sun*, I thought. Then I turned back to the street. It took me less than twenty minutes to cross out of Sidney.

CHAPTER

Twenty

You can always trust a man
wearing a John Deere cap.

Alan Christoffersen's diary

Outside of Sidney there was a lot of road construction and enough detours that at times, even with my map, I wasn't sure if I was walking in the right direction. Kind of like my life. One detour led me to a road that didn't even appear on my map. After an hour of walking along a narrow, two-lane country road, a man pulled up next to me in a red Dodge pickup truck. He was about my age and wore a John Deere cap. He rolled down his window. "You're going the wrong way."

"How do you know that?" I asked.

"The only people going that way, live there. Where are you headed?"

"St. Joseph."

"Yeah, you know that last road you passed—about a half mile back?"

"The dirt one?"

He nodded. "Yeah. You wanted to take that. It's only dirt for about a hundred yards, then it's asphalt again. It runs south and reconnects with 29. I'm going that way, I'd be happy to give you a ride."

"Thank you, but I'm committed to walking."

"Good on ya," he said. "Remember, back a half mile to that dirt road. There's no sign and it breaks up a little bit in places, but don't let it scare you. When you come to a T in the road you're going to want to turn right. That will get you to the 29. Got it?"

"Take a right at the T."

"Perfect."

"Thank you," I said.

"Don't mention it." He rolled up the window then pulled away, spinning a U-turn in front of me. I realized that he had actually gone past his turnoff to help me.

The road the man had directed me to alternated between pavement and dirt but was always surrounded by cornfields. Just as he said, the road led me south, intersecting again with 29, which ran all the way to the Missouri state line.

There wasn't much to see, and my mind wandered. I thought a lot about Analise. I wondered what would become of her. I barely knew her, yet I cared about her. As I pondered this phenomenon I learned something about myself: I've always been a sucker for a damsel in distress. Always. And that included McKale.

Pamela had asked if McKale would have needed me the way she did if she had been a better mother. The question I'd never asked was, would I have been as attracted to McKale if she hadn't needed me? Had I seen McKale in Analise's pain?

I didn't know. I don't think I wanted to. So I forced my mind to other things and just kept walking. Four days later I reached the city of St. Joseph.

CHAPTER

Twenty-one

The man who robs a corner convenience
store is a thief. The man who robs
hundreds is a legend. And the man
who robs millions is a politician.

Alan Christoffersen's diary

St. Joseph was founded in the early 1800s by a fur trader named Joseph Robidoux. In its heyday it was a thriving wilderness outpost—the last stop on the Missouri River, and gateway to the Wild West. It was also the end of the line for west-bound trains.

Today, St. Joseph has a population of over seventy-five thousand residents. The town has several claims to fame, among them that it was the headquarters and starting point for the legendary Pony Express, which sped mail west to those cities inaccessible by rail. It is also the town where the infamous outlaw Jesse James was shot and killed.

Entering St. Joseph, I was struck by the city's beautiful architecture. I walked into the city through an industrial section, then up through suburbs until I reached an area of shopping malls and hotels. I checked into an ambitious hotel called the Stoney Creek Inn, a Western-themed family hotel.

That night I ate at a barbecue joint called the Rib Crib. After looking over the menu I asked my server what the difference was between St. Louis ribs and regular ribs. He replied, "St. Louis ribs have less meat and aren't as good."

"Then I'll have the regular ribs," I said, pretty certain he didn't sell many St. Louis ribs. I ate until I was full, then walked a mile back to my hotel and crashed for the night.

The next morning I decided to see the town's three advertised tourist sites, beginning with the Patee House Museum.

The Patee House was originally built as a 140-room luxury hotel and was, in its day, one of the best-known hotels in the West. It also served as the headquarters for the Pony Express. I was surprised to learn that for all its infamy, the Pony Express only lasted for eighteen months.

Today the Patee House is considered one of the top ten Western museums in the country.

Less than a block away from the Patee House Museum was the home where Jesse James was killed. This wasn't a coincidence. For commercial reasons, the home was lifted from its original site and moved to its current location.

The killing of Jesse James in 1882 made national news. James had been hiding out in St. Joseph under the alias Tom Howard, hoping to start a new life with his wife and two children as a law-abiding citizen. After such a notorious career, and with a lengthy list of enemies, James was understandably paranoid, so he hired two brothers to protect him, Charley and Robert Ford—family friends he believed he could trust.

Unbeknownst to James, Robert Ford had been plotting with the governor to betray the outlaw. One day, while James stood on a chair to right a crooked picture hanging on the wall, Ford shot him in the back of the head.

Then the Ford brothers hurried to the local sheriff to claim the ten-thousand-dollar reward. Much to their surprise, they were arrested for first-degree murder, indicted, and sentenced to death by hanging, all in the same day. Fortunately for the brothers, the governor interceded and pardoned the two men.

History, while heralding the outlaw, has not been as kind to the Ford brothers, painting them as traitors and cowards. After receiving a portion of the reward money, Robert Ford earned a living by posing for photographs in dime museums as "the man who killed Jesse James" and appeared onstage with his brother Charles, reenacting the murder in a touring stage show, which was not well received.

Two years after the killing, Charles, suffering from tuberculosis and addicted to morphine, committed suicide. Robert Ford was killed a few years later by a man who walked up to him in a bar then said, without explanation, "Hello, Bob," and unloaded both barrels of a shotgun into his neck.

As I purchased a book on Jesse James at the home's souvenir counter, I wondered why it is that we humans have such a fascination with outlaws. From Billy the Kid to Al Capone, we have always revered gangsters. Do we do this because it makes us feel good, that we are not that bad—or because deep inside, we're really not that good? Or maybe we're just obsessed with fame—whatever its source.

On the way back to my hotel I stopped at the third most advertised site: The Glore Psychiatric Museum. I wish I hadn't. There was something about the museum that reminded me of those haunted warehouses that pop up in cities every Halloween.

The four-story museum is a collection of horrific, life-sized dioramas, the role of the mentally ill played by mannequins donated by a local department store. The second-floor exhibits follow the history of the treatment of the mentally ill, from witch burnings and devil stompings (the idea being that evil spirits could be stomped out of a person) to the more scientific *Bath of Surprise* (a device not unlike the dunking booths found at today's carnivals, except employing a massive vat of ice water).

There was also a working model of *O'Halloran's Swing*, in which insanity was spun out of the mentally ill who were strapped into the device, which could make up to a hundred revolutions per minute.

On the third floor, the more contemporary exhibits held their own horrors, including mannequins strapped to tables and covered in sheets, lobotomy instruments, a hospital cage, and a fever-cabinet used for heating syphilis patients.

One exhibit displayed the 1,446 items swallowed by a patient, which included 453 nails, 42 screws, a plethora of safety pins, spoons, and salt and pepper shaker tops. The woman died during surgery to remove the items.

Another exhibit showed what the asylum's television repairman discovered: more than five hundred notes crammed into a television set; answers to the questions a patient had been asked by myriad psychiatrists over the years.

The museum seemed to me as schizophrenic as some of those it supposedly championed. On one hand it blared the atrocities of mankind's treatment of the mentally ill, citing that at one time residents of London used to pay to walk through the Bedlam asylum to see those inside chained to walls or strapped to beds. On the other hand it seemed to do precisely that, exploiting the plight of the mentally ill with all the theatrics of a carnival freak show.

After less than a half hour I fled the place and was still upset when I arrived back at my hotel, which was a few miles away. I couldn't sleep so I watched a mindless TV sitcom to erase the memory of what I had seen.

It was time to leave St. Joseph.

CHAPTER

Twenty-two

History bears witness that our
lives are far more influenced by
imagination than circumstance.

Alan Christoffersen's diary

I wrote earlier that small towns are tinder boxes for some of the world's greatest people and ideas. U.S. Route 36 in Missouri may be the most illustrative example of my theory. Along this 160-mile stretch of highway the world was changed. This isn't hyperbole. These are the people who came from the small towns on this one small stretch of American highway:

J. C. Penney

Walt Disney

General John J. Pershing

Mark Twain

And Otto Rohwedder, the inventor of sliced bread.

The day I left St. Joseph, I headed east on Frederick to 29 south, then made my way to the 36.

There were trees everywhere and, according to the book I'd purchased at the Jesse James Home, this was where James and his fellow "bushwhackers" hid out. I spent the night in the small town of Stewartsville (population 759) and ate dinner at the Plain Jane Café.

I started walking early the next morning and by noon I entered Cameron, a city of ten thousand, where I stocked up on supplies. The city of Cameron had a curious birth. In 1854 a group of settlers planned a four-block city called Somerville along the route of the Hannibal to St. Joseph railroad line. As it turned out, Somerville's land was too steep for trains, so the settlers dragged the three buildings of their town a mile southwest and changed the town's name to Cameron.

By twilight I reached Hamilton, the birthplace of J. C. Penney. I walked into the town expecting to find someplace to stay but there was no hotel. I passed by the J. C. Penney Memorial Library and Museum but it was closed for the evening. I bought food at a grocery store called HY-KLAS and camped in a small, overgrown park near the museum.

The next day I walked just shy of twenty-five miles to the town of Chillicothe—the home of sliced bread. They won't let you forget it. It's posted everywhere, from their newspaper's masthead to their city sign: *Welcome to Chillicothe, The Home of Sliced Bread.* Their school mascot is probably a toaster.

I walked all the way into the historic downtown because I saw a sign advertising the Strand Hotel, a big red-brick building that unfortunately had been converted into apartments. Across the street was a beauty salon called *Curl Up & Dye.*

I walked back toward 36, where I had passed a hotel. I ate dinner at a Mexican restaurant called El Toro, then stayed at the Grand River Inn, where a large, white dog of questionable temperament roamed the lobby. It cost fifty dollars. The hotel, not the dog.

The next morning I felt a little dizzy again, but still managed an early start. After twenty miles I turned north off the freeway to the town of Laclede, the hometown of General John "Black Jack" Pershing.

General Pershing had a rather colorful military career,

culminating in the highest rank ever offered a U.S. military leader: *General of the Armies of the United States*, a rank that Congress created especially for him after distinguished service in World War I. No other American soldier ever held such a rank, until 1976, when President Gerald Ford posthumously promoted General George Washington to it.

In addition to his rank, Pershing garnered another unique distinction: he had both a missile and a tank named after him.

Laclede was quiet and picturesque, with streets lined with large elm trees, tidy neighborhoods, and many historic houses and churches. There were no hotels in the town so I continued on to the next, Brookfield, where I stayed at the Travel Inn Motel, advertised as "Veteran Owned and Operated." My room was only thirty-five dollars for the night and had a kitchenette. There was a plethora of Christian literature in the motel's lobby. I picked up a brochure entitled "Why Do We Die?" which I perused on my bed before going to sleep.

The next morning I ate breakfast at the Simply Country Café, then turned south on Main Street to get back to the highway. There was a narrow paved road that paralleled 36 for a few miles and I stayed on that until I reached the turnoff for Marceline—the boyhood home of Walt Disney. I walked three miles from the Marceline exit to reach the small town.

As a boy I had two heroes: Thomas Edison and Walt Disney. When I was growing up in Pasadena, Disneyland was a favorite amusement of mine, and McKale and I had many memories of the park. The first time I publicly put my arms around her was on the Matterhorn ride. It's also where I first called her "Mickey," a nickname that stuck through her entire life.

Elias Disney, Walt's father, had moved his family from Chicago to Marceline in 1906, when young Walter was only four, after two of their neighbor boys had attempted to steal a car and killed a local policeman in a shoot-out.

As a child, Walt spent more time in both Chicago and Kansas City, but Marceline had a far greater impact on his life than any other place the nomadic Disneys landed. Disney spoke of his years in Marceline as his halcyon days and was quoted by a newspaper as saying *"To tell the truth, more things of importance happened to me in Marceline than have happened since, or are likely to in the future."*

I almost passed Disney's boyhood home, a handsome but nondescript house, without recognizing its significance. It was not hard to miss. The home was a private residence, its status as a landmark denoted only by a small sign warning would-be tourists to respect the privacy of the residents.

I stood on the edge of the property and stared at the house, wondering how surprised the town's citizens would have been to know that the little boy who ran the unpaved streets and climbed their trees would someday be known in every corner of the world.

A half hour later I reached the town's main street. I had read that Disneyland's Main Street USA was patterned after Marceline's main street, but in looking at its simple and aging façades, I knew Disney's re-creation was more the offspring of an imaginative memory than a replica of reality.

On Marceline's main street I found a bed-and-breakfast located above the Uptown Theatre, the theater Disney had chosen to premiere *The Great Locomotive Chase* in 1956. The small apartment was decorated with Disney memorabilia and smelled like lemon-scented Pledge. While it lacked the charm of most bed-and-breakfasts, the fact that Disney had been there was enough to justify my stay.

The next morning I walked back to the 36, passing the Disney homestead again on the way out. I had once told McKale that I wanted to visit Marceline some day. I had assumed I would see it with her. I wondered if she knew that I had made it.

CHAPTER

Twenty-three

Today I met a self-described tramp
with a most unfortunate view of God.

Alan Christoffersen's diary

When I saw Israel he was leaning against the railing of the eastbound freeway on-ramp from Marceline, his backpack resting on the ground next to him. He looked like he was in his early to mid thirties; he was short with sandy red hair and wore thick-lensed glasses in round frames. He held a cardboard sign that read:

St. Louis

I nodded at him. "Hey."

"How are you?" he asked cheerfully.

"Fine," I replied. "How are you?"

"Perfect. Beautiful day to be outside."

"Good walking weather," I said.

"Where you headed?" he asked.

"Key West."

"Nice place, Key West," he said, nodding a little. He was the first person I'd told who hadn't reacted with surprise.

"How about you?" I asked.

"Arkansas. I've got a job waiting for me down there."

"What do you do?"

"I'm a roofer."

"That's a long way to go for one house."

He shrugged. "It's what I do—I've been on the road since I was seventeen."

"You've been walking since you were seventeen?"

"No, I don't walk. I'm a tramp."

"Tramps don't walk?"

"Not if we can help it. But it's a nice day. I'd be happy to walk a ways with you, if you don't mind."

"I don't mind," I said.

He fastened his sign to his pack, then pulled it over his

shoulders and walked up to me. The shoulder was wide enough that we could safely walk abreast.

"What's your name?" he asked.

"Alan. Yours?"

"Israel. Israel Campbell."

"And you're a tramp."

"Yes, sir. To regular folk, most homeless people look the same, but we're not." He held his hand out in front of him, extending his index finger. "First, you've got your mountain men—they're easy to spot. They look like they just crawled out of a cave or something. They usually have a lot of facial hair and they only come out in public when they absolutely need something, then go back as soon as they can."

He extended a second finger. "Then you have your crazies. I don't mean serial killer crazy, but just a bit off, you know? Arguing with themselves. You can tell the elevator doesn't quite reach the top floor."

I nodded. "I've seen these people," I said.

He extended a third finger. "Then you got your hobos."

"Hobos and tramps aren't the same thing?"

"No. Hobos give us tramps a bad name."

"How's that?"

"Hobos do a lot of panhandling—you'll see them on off-ramps with cardboard signs begging for money. Tramps don't beg unless we have to. Tramps work. It's a point of pride with us. We just don't have a home or vehicle, so we hitchhike.

"Hobos also ride trains a lot. I do that some, but only if I'm stuck somewhere. There are tricks to the trains. I've been thinking of learning the ropes."

"Tricks? Like what?"

"What I know so far is that it's the pushers, the engines

in the rear, that you want to get into. They've got bottled water, refrigerators, and a bathroom."

"There's no one riding back there?"

"Not usually. But even if someone's in there, they don't necessarily throw you out. Once a guy let me stay on with my dog."

"You have a dog?"

"I did," he said quickly, as if he didn't want to talk about it. "The thing is, they don't really care that much. Having someone ride the train isn't any sweat off their back, but they have to act like they care. You know what I mean?"

I nodded.

"The most important thing is to stay away from the bulls. That's the railroad police. Most of them are lazy and don't bother to search the boxcars, but if they see you, you're in trouble. But, it's like I said, that's mostly hobo stuff. Not that I hate hobos or anything. I'm sociable with anyone on the road. A lot of homeless don't want you around because they don't trust anyone, but I'm not like that. I try to give others money if I have any and I always ask if they're okay. The other day I left two dollars under a bridge and a note that said, 'Have a beer on me. If you don't really need this, leave it for the next guy who does.'"

"So how does one start being a *tramp*?" I asked.

He rubbed his chin. "That's a good question. In my case, it just kind of happened. It's not like I was in career day at school and I said, 'I think I'll be a tramp.' It just kind of snuck up on me. I had a crappy home life, so when I was seventeen, a friend called and said he had some work for me in the next state. I didn't own a car, so I hitchhiked my way there. When I finished the job, someone else called with a job, so I hitchhiked again. Since then I haven't stayed in one place more than three or four months. I guess I'm always looking for greener pastures."

"You're always on the road?"

"If there's work. But not always. Last winter, I dug myself a shelter six feet into the side of a hill. I even had a stove I made of three five-gallon steel buckets. It was kind of a nice place."

"Where are you from originally?" I asked.

"I grew up near St. Louis."

I looked at his sign. "Then you're going home?"

"Not if I can help it. It's just the next big city on my way to Arkansas."

"You still have family in St. Louis?"

"If you call family a bunch of cutthroats who don't care if you're dead or alive. I have no need to see any of them again." He looked down. "So, what are you, hobo or tramp?"

"Neither," I said. "I'm just walking."

"Hitchhiking's faster."

"I'm in no hurry."

He nodded. "Where do you sleep?"

"Depends on the day. A lot of cheap motels. Sometimes in the fields."

"There's a trick to that too," he said. "Ever been hassled by the cops?"

"Not yet. I've been mugged."

He frowned. "Me too. Comes with the territory. But cops have been a bigger problem for me. The most important thing about sleeping on the road is to stay out of sight."

I already knew this, of course, but I didn't tell him as I wanted to hear what he had to say.

"Trees are usually your best bet for cover. I always scope out my sleeping spot from all angles to make sure I can't be seen from the road. I always get up early, usually before the sun, to get back on the road. Nothing worse than having some itchy, tin badge wake you up at three in the morning to tell you to get going, regardless of the weather or how far you're going to have to walk to get to the next exit."

"I haven't had that happen yet," I said.

"You will. Another good place to sleep is under highway overpasses. There's usually a ledge up top that makes a good bunk. Of course, first you need to check to see if someone else has slept there. Most transients leave a trail of beer cans, cardboard, old clothing, you know. If you've been on the road, you've seen it." He shook his head. "Once I found a noose. Thankfully, there wasn't a body attached to it.

"What you've got to do is make sure there isn't any feces. That's the big one. Also, if it's cloudy, I check the ground for water trails, just to make sure that the bridge doesn't leak."

"Thanks for the advice," I said. "So is it hard getting picked up?"

"Sometimes. Like anything, you'll have your days when the fish aren't biting, but not usually. You might say I'm good at it. Hitchhiking is all about psychology. For instance, I used to have a red sleeping bag. I had to get rid of it. Red, yellow, and orange signify danger and people are less likely to pick you up if they see that color. I've never seen like a research study on that, but I tell you, I've proven it.

"The truth is, most of the thinking that goes into picking up a hitchhiker isn't logical. For instance, a lot of people won't pick up a hitchhiker with long hair and a beard because they think he might be a serial killer. You can thank television for that. But it's not the case. Look at Ted Bundy, the Zodiac killer, John Wayne Gacy, Son of Sam, the Green River killer—all of them clean-shaven, respectable-looking guys. So you might say that your best bet of getting picked up is to look like a serial killer." He laughed at this. "Bottom line, if you want a ride, you need to look like you don't need a ride. I always try my best to look presentable. I'd never wear my hair as long as yours. Scares people away."

"Then it's a good thing I'm not hitchhiking," I said.

"Another thing you should know about are truck stops. Truck stops can be lifesavers if you know how to work them. First thing I do when I get to a truck stop is put my pack in the weeds outside so they don't know I'm a hitch-hiker. Then I can blend in with the truckers and sit in the truckers' lounge and warm up or cool down, watch TV, whatever.

"You learn tricks, you know? When truckers fill up at a gas station they get a shower ticket. I can spot them a mile away. I'll ask a guy on the way to his truck if he has an extra shower ticket and most of the time he'll give me one. Sometimes I'll ask the truck stop management for a ticket. I tell them I'm not a panhandler and I'm not going to bother anybody and sometimes they'll just give me a shower ticket.

"But no matter how decent and respectable-looking you keep yourself, some people are still going to look at you like you're a piece of garbage just because they're in a car and you're not. I stopped looking at the people in the cars years ago just to keep from losing my mind. I mean, some people look at you like you're stuck to the bottom of their shoe. I've had people drive by me at forty miles per hour and lock their doors.

"And then there's the head shakers. They look at you waiting on an exit and shake their heads no. It's degrading. I look at their cars, so I don't look like I'm spacing out like a weirdo, but I don't look at the people. There are too many door lockers and head shakers in this world.

"Of course the best way to get a ride is to be a woman. Women can get rides from truckers no problem."

That certainly seemed to be the case with Pamela, I thought.

"Someday I'm going to write a book called *The Psychology of Hitchhiking*. What do you think?"

"I think it sounds interesting," I said.

"You don't know anything about publishing books, do you?"

I shook my head. "Sorry. No."

"Doesn't cost to ask," he said.

We walked a moment in silence.

"Seventeen," I said. "You must get lonely sometimes."

He frowned. "Yeah. Sometimes. I mean, I wish I could find a wife, but finding someone who would live this way isn't very likely. There are women who like the road, but there are ten thousand guys to every one of them, so they get snatched up real quick. Besides, to meet women you have to stay in shelters or ride the trains, and I've never liked either." He sighed a little. "So, what's your story? Why are you on the road?"

I thought briefly about how much to share, then decided to tell him everything. "I lost my wife last year after she broke her back in a horse riding accident. While I was taking care of her, my business was stolen from me. I lost everything. In a matter of weeks I lost my wife, my business, my house, and my cars. All gone. So I packed up and started walking. Key West was as far as I could go without swimming, so that's where I decided to go."

"I'm sorry about all that," he said sympathetically. "There's a lot of bad in this world. What your brother doesn't do to you, God will." He looked around, raising his hands. "It's dog eat dog out there. Those Sunday meeting minions will tell you that God's beauty is witnessed in nature. But their view is selective. The truth is, nature is horrifying, red in tooth and claw." He looked out over the corn. "Out there in that field right now there is death and terror."

"I see a lot of corn to feed people," I said.

"Sure there are sunsets and roses and all that crap, but there's also the fly struggling in the web while a spider sucks the life from it. There are wolves hunting down a baby deer and eating it alive. These things were made by God too."

"You don't get invited to many parties, do you?"

He ignored me. "So what's with this God who makes beautiful sunsets then soaks the ground beneath them in blood. If you ask me, I think God is the ultimate sadist. He's like a kid who drops red ants and black ants together in the same jar just to watch them fight. I think this Earth is nothing more to God than a big cockfight."

"That's about the darkest view of God I've ever heard," I said.

"Welcome to the real world, pal," he said. "People going around saying that God is all just and good, but answer me this: how can God be just when according to almost every religion he damns sinners to an eternity of punishment for something that happens in a finite amount of time? It's not a proportionate response. It's not just and it's certainly not good."

I couldn't answer him.

"Look at it this way. Let's say a kid goes to a store where he sees a candy bar. He has no money, but he really wants that candy. So when he thinks no one is looking, he takes it. He's broken the law. Of course he should pay—I don't disagree with that. But what that poor kid doesn't know is that the store owner has cameras everywhere and all he does is sit back in his office all day waiting to catch someone. So the store owner drags the kid out back behind the store, pours gasoline on him, and lights him on fire. That's your eternal damnation. That's your God. That's your religion."

"That's not my religion," I said. "I don't believe in a God who created us to condemn us. I don't believe that God is fear."

"All religions teach God is fear," Israel said. "Then they dress him up as the good shepherd. A wolf in shepherd's clothing."

"Sometimes good parents use fear," I said. "To protect their children. It's like a mother telling her child not to play in the road, because he might get hit by a car."

"The difference," Israel said, "is that God is the one driving the car."

I nodded. "You're right. That is the difference. You either believe in a God of grace and love or a God of damnation and condemnation, but you can't believe in both, because he can't be the same Being."

"There is no God of grace," Israel said. "You should know. He killed your wife."

"He didn't kill my wife. A horse did."

"He could have stopped her from dying."

"You mean he could have *postponed* her from dying. Because, in the end, everything in this world dies. Everything. That's why people look to God for the next."

Israel looked at me darkly.

"Look," I said. "I don't care what you believe about God. I'm not even sure what I believe. The truth is, much smarter men than us have discussed this question for millennia, and still haven't come to a consensus.

"And as far as the world being *fair* or *good*, the question that baffles me most isn't why bad things happen. In a world like this, I would expect that. What I can't comprehend is why good things happen. Why is there love? Why is there beauty? Why did I love my wife so much? And why did she love me? That's what baffles me. That's what I can't explain."

Israel didn't say anything but continued walking with his head down. After a minute he suddenly stopped walking. "I've bothered you long enough."

I stopped as well. "No bother," I said. "But it was nice talking with you. Travel safe. And good luck with your book. If I ever see it in a store, I'll buy a copy or two."

"Thanks," he said. "I hope you make it to Key West." He shook my hand, then shrugged his pack from his shoulders and sat down on the side of the road with his sign. I just kept on walking.

After Marceline, the towns seemed to change, becoming more Southern. Missouri was always split like that. Even during the Civil War, they weren't sure which side of the conflict they were on.

By the end of the third day from Marceline I entered Monroe City, a quaint town, like Sidney. The houses were well kept with large porches and beautiful yards. It was also the site of the first Civil War battle in northeast Missouri. I learned this from a brochure I picked up at the town's visitors center.

From what I read, the battle was an entertaining affair and the whole of the Monroe citizenry came out in buggies and wagons to picnic and watch the ruckus, which turned out to be a lot more bluster than blood.

The conflict started when a group of Confederate sympathizers gathered in Monroe and Federal troops, led by Colonel Smith, were sent in to break them up. The area was a hotbed of secessionists and Colonel Smith and his men were soon outnumbered and forced to take refuge in a building called the Seminary.

While the pro-secessionist troops surrounded the building, their leader, the Honorable Thomas A. Harris—known to love a good audience—began making a speech to the gathered crowd, who didn't want words, but action.

Harris declared that without a cannon the best thing to do would be retreat and he dismissed his men. His troops declined his offer, and when their cannon arrived the battle resumed. The cannon was a nine-pounder, but the soldiers only had a few nine-pound balls, which they used up with great inefficiency. They then filled their cannon with six-pound balls, which fired so erratically that it dispersed both picnickers *and* Confederate soldiers who said they didn't like being fired on by their own side. By the end of the attack, the pro-South soldiers claimed that the only safe place to be was in front of the cannon.

Federal reinforcements soon arrived to aid Colonel Smith and with one blast of grapeshot from the Union cannon, the secessionists retreated, hiding in buggies and wagons and mingling with the picnickers.

In the meantime, wild rumors of the battle spread and a day after the conflict had ended, Colonel Ulysses S. Grant arrived on the scene with more than two thousand troops. Learning the battle was over, he moved on to Mexico. Thus ended the battle of Monroe.

I passed the Rainbow Motel with a sign outside that read, "Look inside, then decide." I looked inside. I felt as if I'd stepped back into the fifties. An old Pepsi vending machine stood next to the office door and a poster of the Ten Commandments.

I booked a room for the night. The next day I reached Hannibal.

CHAPTER

Twenty-four

Life is not to be found in a cemetery.

Alan Christoffersen's diary

Aside from Disneyland, historic Hannibal was about as magical a town as I could hope to walk through—a storybook hamlet still blessed by its patron saint Samuel Clemens, better known as Mark Twain.

Twain once wrote of his beloved hometown:

> *After all these years I can picture that old time to myself now, just as it was then: the white town drowsing in the sunshine of a summer's morning; the streets empty, or pretty nearly so; one or two clerks sitting in front of the Water Street stores, with their splint-bottomed chairs tilted back against the wall . . . the great Mississippi, the majestic, the magnificent Mississippi, rolling its mile-wide tide along, shining in the sun. . . .*

Walking into Hannibal it is possible to still imagine it as Twain saw it. The city is picturesque, with carefully preserved historic architecture, its eastern panorama framed by the "magnificent" river. It was the kind of place I desperately wanted to share with McKale and wondered why I hadn't.

I checked into the Best Western Plus On the River, which wasn't really *on the river*, although, as a former adman, I could see how they could fudge this—since in 1993 the Mississippi overflowed its banks and flooded the town. So one could claim, in good conscience, that the hotel was, at the time, on the river. Or, more accurately, *in* it.

As the clerk handed me my room key she proudly said, "You might be interested to know that we just got a new treadmill in our exercise room. In case you feel the inclination to walk."

"Thanks," I said. "Good to know."

✦

I ate dinner across the street at a small, shoebox-shaped diner, Hannibal fried chicken with biscuits and sawmill gravy, then returned to the hotel to soak in the hot tub. I read a little of my Jesse James book, then retired early.

Being in Hannibal lifted my spirits, and, perhaps for the first time since I left Seattle, I felt more like a tourist than a man on a pilgrimage. The next morning I went for a walk around the town, stopping for breakfast and coffee at the Java Jive on Main Street. My waitress was one of the most beautiful women I had ever seen. I guessed her to be in her early to mid twenties, but she was dressed in retro clothing: a formfitting striped dress with a red beret and sash and high-heeled shoes. She reminded me of one of those girls that B-52 bomber squads painted on the noses of their flying coffins.

The pastry and coffee were good and I leisurely drank my coffee, the tourist traffic outside as meandering as the river the town parallels. It was a pleasure to watch others walk for a change.

I hadn't planned on spending the day in Hannibal, but an hour into the morning I knew I would. After finishing my second coffee I walked north to see Twain's home.

The Mark Twain historic complex was well preserved with cobblestone streets closed off to automobile traffic. Among the buildings still standing are Twain's boyhood home, complete with the white fence Tom Sawyer hoodwinked the neighbor boys into painting, and the reconstructed home of Tom Blankenship—the boy *Huckleberry Finn* was based on. Twain wrote of his friend Tom:

*His liberties were totally unrestricted. He was the only re-
ally independent person—boy or man—in the community,
and by consequence he was tranquilly and continuously
happy, and was envied by all the rest of us. We liked him;
we enjoyed his society. And as his society was forbidden us
by our parents, the prohibition trebled and quadrupled its
value, and therefore we sought and got more of his society
than of any other boy's.*

There was also Twain's father's justice of the peace office and the home of Laura Hawkins, the neighbor girl on
whom Twain had based the character Becky Thatcher. In
this, the author and I shared common ground—both of
our lives were forever changed by the girl next door.

After touring the homes, I walked south along the bank
of the Mississippi until I came to the loading plank of the
Mark Twain riverboat. I paid fifteen dollars for a one-hour
cruise and boarded the craft.

The boat didn't cover much ground, or water, just pad-
dling up the river a spell then back down, but the ride was
as pleasant and smooth as a southern drawl.

Steve, the riverboat captain, was a jovial host and as
we pulled away from the dock, he sang out over the boat's
PA system an obligatory "Maaaark Twaaaaaaain," reassur-
ing us that the water was two fathoms deep, which to the
riverboat pilot meant safe water. Safe water. It is still a
comforting reassurance to us today.

I climbed up to the boat's wheelhouse and asked Captain Steve something I'd always wondered: why were the
top of the boat's smokestacks fluted?

"Mostly tradition," he replied. "But back in Twain's day
the flutes helped keep the embers from the boat's furnace
from falling on the passengers' heads."

Satisfied with the answer I went back to the ship's bow and drank a Coke.

On our return to shore, the captain blew the boat's powerful steam whistle thrice before sidling up to the dock. I thanked Captain Steve and disembarked, then walked to Main Street, ate lunch at Ole Planters Restaurant, then wandered back to my hotel, perusing store windows on the way.

Two blocks from my hotel I passed an office with a sign in the window that read:

Haunted Hannibal Ghost Tours

I went inside to check it out. No one was inside, but there was a sign-up list for the evening's tour. I added my name to the list.

Just about everything in Hannibal is haunted, and everyone in town had a ghost story they were eager to share. The first ghost story I heard was shared that morning by my waitress over breakfast. The renter in an apartment next to the Java Jive kept complaining about the creepy organ music that woke him every night at 3 A.M. He refused to believe that the coffeehouse management was not to blame even though the coffeehouse didn't own an organ and closed at midnight.

Even the public library had stories of a fastidious apparition who, after closing hours, threw books on the floor that had been incorrectly reshelved.

After a nap at the hotel, I woke feeling a little dizzy again, but it soon passed. I ate dinner at the same diner I had the night before, then walked two blocks to the shop where I'd signed up for the ghost tour.

A long, gray passenger van was idling in front of the office and a small congregation on the sidewalk. I walked inside the office. A tall, pleasant-looking woman with long, dishwater blond hair stood next to the counter holding a clipboard.

"I'm here for the ghost tour," I said.

"Then you've come to the right place," she said, wagging a pen in front of me. "You must be Mr. Christoffersen."

"That's me," I said.

She marked the list on her clipboard. "I'm Doreen. You're alone, right?"

I felt it accutely. "Right."

"Just go ahead and find a seat in the van out front."

I walked back outside. The small group I'd passed on the way in was now seated inside the van. The van's door was wide open.

There were five of us in the group: a young, fresh-faced couple who, from their glassy-eyed expressions, I guessed to be honeymooners, occupied half the front bench, and two women in their mid fifties sat in the middle row.

The driver was a thin, thirtyish man with a face shadowed with stubble. Even though it was already getting dark he wore Ray-Ban aviators, and he looked a little like Richard Petty, the former NASCAR champion. His head was bowed as he was evidently playing a game on his cell phone.

"Good evening," I said as I climbed into the vehicle. Only the ladies greeted me back. The driver was fixated on his phone and the couple was still fixated on each other, oblivious to all other life on the planet. I squeezed through to the backseat of the van.

A few minutes later, Doreen poked her head in through the front passenger window. "We're waiting for one more."

The driver grunted and scratched his face, but still

didn't look up. About two minutes later Doreen returned. She was standing next to an elderly gentleman who wore a flat cap and gray sweater and carried a black, metal-tipped cane.

"There you are, Mr. Lewis," Doreen said. "I'll take your cane. Watch your step."

Mr. Lewis was probably in his mid to late eighties, gray and bent with age. He struggled to climb up into the front row, sitting next to the honeymooners. Doreen helped him fasten his seat belt, then slid the side door shut and climbed into the front passenger seat. When she was settled, she turned around and smiled at us.

"Welcome, everyone, to haunted Hannibal. I have been guiding this tour for nearly twelve years now, and let me tell you, in those years I've seen some amazing things. Rest assured, your experiences on this tour are your own. We don't judge the validity of your encounters, we just accept and let things happen. Most of all, you're going to have a good time.

"Our first stop tonight is rife with paranormal activity: the Old Baptist Cemetery." She turned to the driver. "Let's go."

The driver put down his phone, then looked over his shoulder and pulled out into the quiet, vacant street.

The cemetery was about five minutes from our pickup point and the last of the day's light was gone when the van stopped. Doreen and the driver helped Mr. Lewis out of the van, then the rest of us followed.

I was the last one out and the small group had already formed a half circle in front of Doreen. Most of the cemetery was draped beneath a canopy of aged oak trees, which left us standing in a darker shade of night.

Doreen handed each of us copper rods that swiveled

in wooden handles, like divining rods, the kind water witches use to find water.

"This little device will help you find spectral energy," she said. "As you walk through the cemetery, hold the rods in front of you like this." She demonstrated, holding the rods in front of her with both hands like she was holding a pair of guns. "If they start crossing, you might have found someone who wants to communicate with you. Sometimes the lines will just open up. I've even seen them spin. Go ahead and ask the spirits questions. The ghosts up here are used to us, so they know what to do. But do be careful, it's dark, so watch where you're stepping. We don't want anyone tripping over anything. Now off you go. Have fun!"

At Doreen's dismissal, everyone wandered off with their spirit wands, headed toward different sections of the cemetery. I stood there feeling stupid, holding the pointers in front of me.

Mr. Lewis was still next to me. He was moving slowly, his cane in one hand, both of the rods in the other. I thought that at his age, traipsing around cemeteries at night might be a bit too ambitious.

"Are you all right?" I asked.

"Certainly," he said curtly, his voice low and gravelly.

"Have you done this before?"

"Countless times."

"Oh," I said, a little surprised. "Have you ever encountered anything?"

"Not what I'm looking for." He turned and looked at me, his eyes as dark as the cemetery. "I'm looking for my wife."

His response jarred me. I had never considered looking for McKale in this way. Nor did I want to. Everything about it seemed wrong.

"You've been looking for her for a while?"

"Yes," he said. Then he hobbled away, mumbling something as he crossed the grounds.

I walked off alone toward the cemetery's northeast corner, holding the rods in front of me. About ten minutes later, Doreen joined me. "How's it going?" she asked.

"Fine," I said.

"Good," she said brightly.

Nothing had happened, except the rods had moved a little, something that was almost impossible to prevent, even if you were trying.

"Tell me," I said. "What do you know about Mr. Lewis?"

"Mr. Lewis is a retired insurance salesman from Tulsa, Oklahoma. His wife died a while back and since then he's spent most of his time traveling the country to séances and ghost tours, looking for proof that she still exists."

"Has he had any luck?" I asked.

"Apparently not. A lot of people have claimed to find her, but none have passed his test."

"What's his test?"

"He had a pet name he called her. If they can't tell him what it is, he knows it's not her."

"When you say a while, how long are we talking about? A few years?"

Her eyebrows rose. "Try forty."

"Forty years," I said. "He's been traveling the country for forty years looking for his wife?"

She nodded. "He's spent his life and fortune trying to find her. At least that's what he told me when he signed up for the tour."

"Doesn't he have any family?"

"He has four adult children. Sounds like he's estranged from them. I guess he was pretty broken up about losing her." Doreen read the look of disapproval on my face, then said, "I know, I wouldn't do it. But you can't judge someone until you've walked in their moccasins, can you? So have *you* found anyone tonight?"

"Not yet," I said.

"Well let's get busy," she said.

For the next half hour Doreen followed me around the cemetery looking for traces of paranormal activity. My lines crossed several times—actually, several dozen times—and, at Doreen's encouragement, I found myself in a one-sided conversation with a grave marker named Mary Stewart. My divining rods had rotated backward and Doreen was certain that Mary's spirit was hugging me.

I'll admit to one peculiar phenomenon. I kept feeling the sensation of walking through spiderwebs, even when I was out in the open.

An hour later as we reboarded the van, the two women were chatting excitedly, one claiming she'd found a spirit who knew her recently deceased grandmother. The honeymooners were still just staring at each other, clearly desperate to get back to the hotel.

Mr. Lewis was the last to return, only doing so at Doreen's insistence. As he struggled into the van he looked sad or angry, I couldn't really tell which, as his face was sufficiently hard that it was difficult to read any emotion except unhappiness. Watching him had a powerful effect on me.

The van took a circuitous route back to Doreen's office, passing by a series of buildings that were supposedly haunted, including the Old Catholic Church, which was up for sale. Doreen told us that one of her clients claimed to have placed a recorder in the church and, within minutes, recorded the sound of an invisible choir.

A few blocks past the Old Church, Doreen pointed out a Victorian home. "Up ahead here, to your left, is LaBinnah Bistro. I recommend that you eat there if you get the chance. Can anyone figure out where the restaurant got its name?"

We all looked out at the building, even the honeymooners.

"It's French," one of the women said.

"Or Cajun," said the other.

"No, that's not it," Doreen said.

"It was the chef's wife's name," the male honeymooner said, the first word he'd spoken to anyone *but* his wife.

"No," Doreen said.

"I know," I said.

Doreen looked at me. "You think you do?"

"*LaBinnah* is *Hannibal* spelled backwards."

Doreen clapped. "You're the first person in twelve years who's gotten that right," she said. "Twelve years."

When we'd returned to the office and disembarked from the van, Doreen asked me what I'd thought of the tour. "It was life changing," I said.

She beamed at my report. "I'm so pleased. Thank you for coming. And come back soon."

"Good night," I said, then turned and walked back to my hotel.

I meant what I said to Doreen, just not for the reasons she had likely assumed. The experience had had a profound impact on me. Not the paranormal aspect of the tour—which I had found mildly amusing—but rather my experience with Mr. Lewis. In this man I had seen something far more frightening than any graveyard specter or poltergeist. I had seen the bitterness of unaccepted loss. I had seen the possibility of my own future and my own ruin.

CHAPTER

Twenty-five

What's wrong with me? Something's broken.

Alan Christoffersen's diary

A man's experiences of life are a book. There was never yet an uninteresting life. Such a thing is an impossibility. Inside of the dullest exterior there is a drama, a comedy, and a tragedy.

—Mark Twain

I hated to leave Hannibal. On the way out of town, I stopped at Mark Twain's Cave, the same cave Twain explored as a boy and referenced in five of his books—most famously in *The Adventures of Tom Sawyer*, where Tom and Becky get mixed up with Injun Joe.

I left my pack behind the counter at the cave's gift shop, then entered the cave with a tall, boyish-looking guide and a small group from a Church of God Bible class visiting from Memphis, Tennessee.

Mark Twain's cave was a remarkable thing—a labyrinth of shelved limestone that tangled and twisted in the belly of the hill for more than six miles.

"One could get more lost in here than on the New Jersey Turnpike," our guide announced. How he had come up with that exact comparison I wasn't sure. I decided that he'd probably been lost in New Jersey at some time.

For the next hour we wound our way through a few dozen of the cave's more than 260 passages. Inside, the cave was chilly, as it maintained a year-round temperature of 52 degrees, and many in our group complained that they hadn't brought their sweaters.

Among the many things we saw was the signature of Jesse James, who hid out in the cave after the robbery of a train in a nearby town.

Our guide led us to Grand Avenue, the largest room in the cave, where Tom and Becky were lost in darkness after a bat doused Becky's candle. This story was, of course, a natural segue into the climax of the tour (of all cave tours, for that matter) when our guide turned out the lights with the exhortation, "Put your hand up to your face and see if you can see it."

We couldn't, of course. "Dark as sin," McKale would have said. Actually she never would have come in the cave; she was crazily claustrophobic. Amusingly, someone said "ouch" after hitting himself in the nose.

Our guide turned the lights back on then said, "Let me share with you an interesting fact. The human eye needs light to survive. If you got lost in this cave, you would be permanently blind in six to eight weeks."

"Imagine that," the woman next to me said. "That would be horrible."

"If you got lost in this cave, you'd be dead long before you went blind," I said.

"Oh," she said. "I hadn't thought of that." Peculiarly, the woman smiled, as if this were a comforting thought.

Our guide continued. "At one time this cave was owned by a Hannibal doctor named Joseph Nash McDowell, who bought the cave to do 'scientific' experiments with mummification. When his daughter died, he brought her in and embalmed her. He did his experiments in that crevice about fifty yards back."

"Wait," I said. "He did experiments with his daughter's corpse?"

"Yes, sir," the guide said.

I shook my head. Just when you think people couldn't get any more bizarre, a Joseph Nash McDowell turns up.

At the completion of the tour I retrieved my pack, then started back to historic Hannibal. That wasn't my original plan. I had stopped at the cave on my way to highway 79, a scenic route that followed the Mississippi River south along the Missouri–Illinois border. But as I verified my route with a clerk at the cave's gift shop, I learned that the river had recently washed out the road and the highway was closed. I reasoned that I could always walk around construction crews, but the clerk wasn't sure that was possible. Considering that a closed route might mean backtracking for days, I decided not to take the chance.

My only other option was to take U.S. Route 61 southeast to St. Louis. It would be a considerably busier route but I really had no other choice.

Over the next three days, I passed through New London, Frankford, Bowling Green, Eolia, and Troy. I woke in Troy feeling dizzy and nauseous again, but forced it aside, vowing to rest properly once I reached St. Louis.

I had had a headache all day, and about six miles from the 70 junction into St. Louis, my vertigo returned with a vengeance. Oddly, my first thought was that there was an earthquake, as the spinning was much worse than before. I staggered then fell, landing partially on my pack, which cushioned my fall. I rolled to my stomach and began violently vomiting, struggling to hold myself upright as my head throbbed with pain. *What was happening to me?*

"McKale," I groaned. It's the last thing I remember before passing out.

CHAPTER

Twenty-six

Déjà vu.

Alan Christoffersen's diary

I woke in the hospital. I couldn't believe that I was in a hospital again—it was the third time since I'd left Seattle. I hadn't been in a hospital that many times in my entire life. The room was dim and I could hear the beeping and whirring of machines. I looked over at my arm. It was bruised and there was an IV taped to it.

"It's about time you woke," a voice said. I looked over to see a young, African-American nurse standing to the side of the room reading a machine.

"Where am I?"

"You are at the St. Louis University Hospital."

"How did I get here?"

"I don't know," she said. "I wasn't here when you arrived. Do you remember anything?"

"I was just walking, when I suddenly got dizzy and everything started to spin. I must have blacked out." I looked at her. "What's wrong with me?"

"I'll leave that to the doctor to talk to you about," she said. "In the meantime, there's someone here to see you."

I couldn't imagine who it could be. "I don't know anyone around here."

"Well, she knows you. She's been in the waiting room for three hours. I'll send her in." She walked out of the room.

I stared at the door, wondering who could possibly be here to see me. Falene suddenly appeared in the doorway.

"Hi," she said sweetly.

"Falene. What are you doing here?"

She walked to the side of my bed. "The police called me. I was the last number you dialed on your cell phone."

". . . You came all this way?"

"Of course I did. You needed me." I noticed that her

eyes were red, as if she'd been crying. A tear rolled down her cheek.

"What's wrong?" I asked.

She shook her head.

"What is it, Falene?"

The tears fell faster. She furtively wiped her eyes then looked away from me.

"Falene . . ."

She reached over and took my hand. Her hand felt soft and warm. "Your father will be here soon," she said. "Can he tell you?"

"Is it bad?"

She just stared at me, tears rolling down her cheeks.

I looked down for a moment, then I said, "When McKale was hurt, you called me. When Kyle stole my business, you called me. You've always told me the truth, no matter how hard. I'd rather hear it from you."

She wiped her eyes. "Oh, Alan," she said.

"Please. What's wrong with me?"

She looked into my eyes, her eyes welling up in tears. "They found a brain tumor."

E P I L O G U E

To learn grace is to discover God.

Alan Christoffersen's diary

Who am I? Or perhaps a better question is, what am I? A refugee? A fugitive? A saunterer? Henry David Thoreau, in his essay on walking, wrote that the word *sauntering* was derived from "people who roved about the country in the Middle Ages under pretense of going *à la Sainte Terre*," to the Holy Land, till the children exclaimed, " 'There goes a Sainte-Terrer,' a Saunterer—a Holy-Lander." Maybe this is the truest definition of who I am—a Pilgrim. My walk is my pilgrimage. And, like all worthwhile pilgrimages, mine too is a journey from *wretchedness* to *grace*. Grace. I have learned much on my walk, but most recently, I have learned of grace.

As a boy, I heard my mother sing "Amazing Grace." She said grace over meals and praised all graciousness. My father, on the other hand, rarely spoke the word, relegating it to Sunday vernacular, with little use in an accountant's calculated life. But he showed grace through his actions, by caring for me the best he could even when his own heart was broken.

For most of my life I have thought of grace as a hope of a bright tomorrow in spite of the darkness of today—and this is true. In this way we are all like Pamela, walking a road to grace—hoping for mercy. What we fail to realize is that grace is more than our destination, it is the journey itself, manifested in each breath and with each step we take. Grace surrounds us, whirls about us like the wind, falls on us like rain. Grace sustains us on our journeys, no matter how perilous they may be and, make no mistake, they are all perilous. We need not hope for grace, we merely need to open our eyes to its abundance. Grace is all around us, not just in the hopeful future but in the miracle of now.

And, if we travel well, we will become as grace and

learn the lesson meant from the journey, not to dismiss error, but to eagerly forgive the err-er, to generously share the balm of mercy and love for, before the eyes of Heaven, we all walk as fools. And the more we exercise our portion of grace, the better we receive it. The abundance of this grace is only limited by ourselves, as we cannot receive that which we are not willing to accept—be it for ourselves or others.

It's been written that, *He who does not forgive is guilty of the greater sin.* That verse had always confounded me. I had considered it unjust at best and cruel at worst. But these words were not meant as condemnation—rather as illumination of an eternal truth: that to not extend forgiveness is to burn the bridge that we ourselves must cross.

I have found grace in my walk. I saw it in the joy of Pamela's freedom, in the hope in Analise's eyes, and in the forgiving heart of Leszek. I found it in Washington in the wisdom of Ally and the friendship of Nicole, and walking through Idaho in the gratitude of Kailamai. And even now, in my moment of uncertainty and fear, I see it in the presence of Falene. Grace is all around me. It always has been. How could I have been so blind?

I am still in the hospital. My father arrived a few hours after I woke. Tests have been done, and, no doubt, there will be myriad more to come. We do not yet know if my tumor is malignant or benign, and whether or not it has spread. I know only enough to fear. I fear death, as any sane man does, but I'm a creative man so my fears are greater than most.

Still, part of me—a dark or light part I'm not yet certain—hungers for death's sleep, perhaps to wake in the brightness and warmth of McKale's arms. This might seem a fool's hope—to seek love in death—but, truthfully, I do not know where McKale is *but* death.

I don't know. Not since I set out from Seattle has my journey been more uncertain. I don't know if or when I will be walking again. I do not know whether or not I will reach Key West. But this much I know—whether I accept the journey or not, the road will come. The road always comes. The only question any of us can answer, is how we will choose to meet it.

Coming Spring 2013, book 4 of The Walk series

To learn more about The Walk
series or to join Richard's mailing list and
receive special offers and information please visit:
www.richardpaulevans.com

Join Richard on Facebook at the
Richard Paul Evans fan page
www.facebook.com/RPEfans

Or write to him at:
P.O. Box 712137 • Salt Lake City, Utah • 84171

*R*ichard Paul Evans is the author of the number-one bestselling novel *The Christmas Box*. Each of his novels has appeared on the *New York Times* bestseller list; there are more than 14 million copies of his books in print. His books have been translated into more than twenty-five languages, and several have been international bestsellers. He has won two first-place *Storytelling World* Awards for his children's books and the *Romantic Times* Best Women's Novel of the Year Award. Evans received the *Washington Times* Humanitarian of the Century Award and the Volunteers of America National Empathy Award for his work helping abused children. Evans lives in Salt Lake City with his wife, Keri, and their five children.